THE
CHRISTMAS
DOG

THE
CHRISTMAS
DOG

Melody Carlson

Recycling programs
for this product may
not exist in your area.

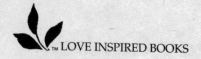 LOVE INSPIRED BOOKS

ISBN-13: 978-0-373-78870-5

The Christmas Dog

Love Inspired Books / October 2014

First published by Revell, a division of Baker Publishing Group

Copyright © 2009 by Melody Carlson

www.Harlequin.com

Printed in U.S.A.

MELODY CARLSON

is the prolific author of more than two hundred books, including fiction, nonfiction, and gift books for adults, young adults and children. She is also the author of *Three Days, The Gift of Christmas Present, The Christmas Bus, An Irish Christmas,* and *All I Have to Give.* Her writing has won several awards, including a Gold Medallion for *King of the Stable* (Crossway, 1998) and a Romance Writers of America RITA® Award for *Homeward* (Multnomah, 1997). She lives with her husband in Sisters, Oregon. Visit her website at www.melodycarlson.com.

Chapter One

As Betty Kowalski drove home from church on Sunday, she realized she was guilty of two sins. First of all, she felt envious—perhaps even lustful—of Marsha Deerwood's new leather jacket. But, in Betty's defense, the coat was exquisite. A three-quarter-length jacket, it was beautifully cut, constructed of a dove-gray lambskin, and softer than home-made butter. Betty knew this for a fact since she had touched the sleeve of Marsha's jacket and audibly sighed just as Pastor Gordon had invited the congregation to rise and bow their heads in prayer.

"It's an early anniversary present from Jim," Marsha had whispered after the pastor proclaimed a hearty "Amen." As usual, the two old friends sat together in the third pew from the front. On Marsha's other side, next to the aisle so he could help with the collection plates, sat Marsha's husband, James Deerwood, a recently retired physician and respected member of the congregation.

Naturally Betty didn't show even the slightest sign of jealousy. Years of practice made this small performance no great challenge. Instead, Betty simply smiled, complimented Marsha on the lovely garment, and pretended not to notice the worn cuffs of her own winter coat, a charcoal-colored Harris Tweed that had served her well for several decades now. Still, it was classic and timeless, and a new silk scarf or a pair of sleek leather gloves might dress it up a bit. Not that she could afford such little luxuries right now. Besides, she did not care to dwell on such superficialities (especially during the service). Nor would she want anyone to suspect how thoughts such as these distracted her while Pastor Gordon preached with such fiery intensity about the necessity of loving one's neighbors today. He even pounded his fist on the pulpit a couple of times, something the congregation rarely witnessed in their small, dignified church.

But now, as Betty drove her old car toward

her neighborhood, she was mindful of Pastor Gordon's words. And thus she became cognizant of her second sin. Not only did Betty *not* love her neighbor, she was afraid that she hated him wholeheartedly. But then again, she reminded herself, it wasn't as if Jack Jones lived *right* next to her. He wasn't her *next-door* neighbor. Not that it made much difference, since only a decrepit cedar fence separated their backyards. It was, in fact, that rotten old fence that had started their dispute in the first place.

"This fence is encroaching on my property," Jack had said to her in October. She'd been peacefully minding her own business, enjoying the crisp sunny day as she raked leaves in her backyard.

"What do you mean?" She set her bamboo rake aside and went over to hear him better, which wasn't easy since his music, as usual, was blaring.

"I mean I've studied the property lines in our neighborhood, and that fence is at least eight feet into my yard," he said.

"That fence is on your property line, fair and square." She looked him straight in the eyes. "It's the public access strip that's—"

"No way!" He pointed toward the neigh-

boring yards where the public access strip
had been split right down the middle. "See
what I mean? Your yard has encroached over
the whole public access strip and—"

"Excuse me," she said, shaking her finger
at him like he was in grade school. "But the
original owners agreed to build that fence
right where it is. No one has encroached on
anyone."

He rubbed his hand through his straggly
dark hair, jutted out his unshaved chin, narrowed his eyes. "It's over the line, lady."

Betty did not like being called "lady." But
instead of losing her temper, she pressed her
lips together tightly and mentally counted to
ten.

"And it's falling down," he added.

"Well," she retorted, "since it's on your
property, I suggest you fix it." As she turned
and walked away, she felt certain that he increased the volume on his music just to spite
her. It seemed clear the battle lines were
drawn.

Fortunately, the weather turned cold after
that. Consequently, Betty no longer cared to
spend time in her backyard, and her windows
remained tightly closed to shut out Jack's
noise and music.

Now Betty tightened her grip on the steering wheel, keeping her gaze straight ahead as she drove down Persimmon Lane, the street on which Jack lived. She did not want that insufferable young man to observe her looking his way. Although it was hard *not* to stare at the run-down house with the filthy red pickup truck parked right on the front lawn. Obviously, the old vehicle couldn't be parked in the driveway. That space was buried in a mountain of junk covered with ugly blue tarps, which were anchored with old plastic milk bottles. She assumed the bottles were filled with dirty water, although another neighbor (who suspected their young neighbor was up to no good) had suggested the mysterious brown liquid in the containers might be a toxic chemical used in the manufacturing of some kind of illegal drugs.

Betty sighed and continued her attempt to avert her gaze as she slowed down for the intersection of her street, Nutmeg Lane. But despite her resolve, she glanced sideways and let out a loud groan. Oh, to think that the Spencer house had once been the prettiest home in the neighborhood!

As she turned the corner, she remembered how that house used to look. For years it had been painted a lovely sky-blue with clean white trim, and the weed-free lawn had always been neatly cut and perfectly edged. The flower beds had bloomed profusely with annuals and perennials, and Gladys Spencer's roses had even won prizes at the county fair. Who ever would've guessed it would come to this?

The original owners, Al and Gladys Spencer, had taken great pride in their home. And they had been excellent neighbors and wonderful friends for decades. But over the past five years, the elderly couple had suffered a variety of serious health problems. Gladys had gone into a nursing home, then Al had followed her, and eventually they both passed away within months of each other. The house had sat vacant for a few years.

Then, out of the blue, this Jack character had shown up and taken over. Without saying a word to anyone, he began tearing into the house as if he was intent on destroying it. And even when well-meaning neighbors tried to meet him or find out who he was, he made it perfectly clear that he had absolutely no interest in speaking to any of them. He was a rude young man and didn't care who knew it.

As Betty pulled into her own driveway, she

wondered not for the first time if Jack Jones actually owned that house. No one had ever seen a For Sale sign go up. And no one had witnessed a moving van arrive. Her secret suspicion was that Jack Jones was a squatter.

It had been late last summer when this obnoxious upstart took occupancy of the house, and according to Penny Horton, the retired schoolteacher who lived next door, the scruffy character had brought only a duffle bag and three large plastic crates with him. But the next day, without so much as a howdy-do, he began tearing the house apart. Penny, who was currently in Costa Rica, was the one who informed Betty of the young man's name, and only because she discovered a piece of his mail that had been delivered mistakenly to her mailbox. "It looked like something official," Penny had confided to Betty. "It seemed to be from the government. Do you suppose he's in the witness protection program?" *Or perhaps he's out on parole*, Betty had wanted to suggest, but had kept these thoughts to herself.

Out of concern, Betty had attempted to reach the Spencers' daughter, Donna, by calling the old number that was still in her little blue address book. But apparently that number had been changed, and the man who answered the phone had never heard of anyone by that name. Even when Betty called information, citing the last town she knew Donna had lived in, she came up empty-handed. So she gave up.

Betty frowned as she bent to open her old garage door. The wind was blowing bitter and cold now, and she had forgotten her wool gloves in the car but didn't want to go back for them. She didn't usually park in the garage, but the weatherman had predicted unusually low temperatures, and her car's battery was getting old. She gripped the cold metal handle on the single-car garage door and, not for the first time, longed for a garage-door opener—like the one Marsha and Jim had on their triple-car garage. One simply pushed the remote's button and the door magically went up, and once the car was inside, down the door went again. How she wished for one now.

Her grandmother's old saying went through her head as she struggled to hoist up the stubborn door. "If wishes were fishes, we'd all have a fry." Oh, yes, wouldn't she!

Betty shivered as she got back into her car. She still couldn't get that obnoxious neighbor out of her head—all thanks to this morning's sermon! But what was she supposed to do? How could she love someone so despicable? How was it even possible? Oh, she'd heard that with God all things were possible…but this?

She decided to commit the dilemma to prayer. She bowed her head until it thumped the top of the steering wheel, asking God to help her love her loathsome neighbor and to give her the strength she lacked. "Amen," she said. Then she tried to focus her full attention on carefully navigating her old Buick forward into the snug garage, although she was still thinking about that thoughtless Jack Jones— if that was his real name.

The next thing she knew, she heard a loud scratching sound and realized she'd gotten too close to the right side of the garage door. She took in a sharp breath and quickly backed up, readjusted the wheel, and went forward again, but when she turned off her engine, she knew it was too late. The damage was done. And, really, wasn't this also Jack Jones's fault? He was a bad egg—and had probably been one from the very beginning.

As Betty sat there, unwilling to get out and see what the scrape on her car looked like, she replayed the man's list of faults. And they were many. Right from the start, he'd stepped on people's toes. With absolutely no consideration for his neighbors' ears or sleeping habits, he had used his noisy power tools in the middle of the night and played his music loudly during the day. Of course, these habits weren't quite so obnoxious when winter came and everyone kept their windows shut. But how many times had Betty gotten up for her late-night glass of milk only to observe strange lights and flashes going on behind Jack's closed blinds? Sometimes she worried that Jack's house was about to go up in flames, and perhaps the whole neighborhood along with it. She would ponder over what that madman could possibly be doing. And why did he need to do it at night? What if it was something immoral or illegal? For all she knew, Jack Jones could be a wanted felon who was creating bombs to blow up things like the county courthouse or even the grade school.

Betty removed her keys from the ignition and reached for her purse and Bible. She slowly got out of the car, and out of habit ever since that notorious Jack Jones had moved into the neighborhood, she securely locked her car's doors. Then she sat her purse and Bible on the hood of the car and peeked around the right side to see the front fender. The horizontal gash was about a foot long with a hook on one end, causing it, strangely enough, to resemble the letter J. Betty just shook her head. It figured…*J* for Jack.

So she continued to obsess over him—and over today's sermon and her futile prayer. How *was* it possible to love someone so completely disagreeable and inconsiderate and downright evil? She grunted as she struggled to lower the garage door. *Really,* she thought as she stood up straight, *even Pastor Gordon would be singing a different tune if he was forced to live next to Jack Jones.*

Betty let herself into the house, turning the deadbolt behind her—another habit she had never felt the need to do before Jack Jones had entered the picture. She set her purse and Bible on the kitchen table, then went to the sink and just stood there. She gazed blankly out the window. It was a bleak time of year with bare trees, browning grass, dead leaves—all in sepia tones. A nice coat of snow would make it look much prettier.

But she wasn't looking at her own yard. Her eyes were fixed on her neighbor's backyard. As usual, it looked more like a dump site than a delightful place where flowers once flourished and children once played. The dilapidated deck was heaped with black plastic trash bags filled with only God knew what. And as if that were not bad enough, there were pieces of rubbish and rubble strewn about. But the item that caught Betty's eye today, the thing that made her blink, was the pink toilet!

Betty recognized this toilet as the one that had once graced Gladys Spencer's prized guest bathroom. It had been a small, tidy bathroom with pink and black tiles, a pink sink, and a matching toilet. Betty had used it many a time when she'd joined Gladys and their friends for bridge club or baby showers or just a neighborly cup of coffee. Gladys had always taken great pride in her dainty pink guest soaps and her pink fingertip towels with a monogrammed *S* in silver metallic thread.

As Betty stared at that toilet, so forlorn and out of place in the scruffy backyard, she realized that time had definitely moved on. Betty could relate to that toilet on many levels. She too was old and outdated. She too felt unnecessary…and perhaps even unwanted.

Betty shook her head in an attempt to get rid of those negative thoughts. Then she frowned to see that last night's high winds must've pushed the deteriorating fence even further over into what once had been the Spencers' yard. Jack Jones would not be the least bit pleased about that. Not that she cared particularly.

Betty had long since decided that the fence, whether it was her responsibility or his, could wait until next summer to resolve. But if she could have her way, she would erect a tall, impenetrable stone wall between the two properties.

She filled her old stainless teakettle and tried to remember happier days—a time when she'd been happy to live in her house. She thought back to when Chuck was still alive and when they'd just moved into their new house in Gary Meadows. It had seemed like a dream come true. Finally, after renting and saving for eight years, they were able to afford a home of their own. And it was brand-new!

Al and Gladys Spencer had immediately befriended Chuck and Betty as well as their two small children with a dinner of burgers and baked beans. And that's when the two men began making plans to build a fence. "Good fences make good neighbors," Al said.

Since Chuck and Betty's children were still young, whereas Al and Gladys had only one child still at home who was about to graduate, it was decided that they'd put the fence directly on the Spencers' property line, allowing the Kowalskis the slightly larger yard. "And less mowing for me," Al joked. And since the city had no plans to use the public access strip, and there was no alley, it had all been settled quite simply and congenially. That is, until Jack Jones moved in.

Not for the first time, Betty thought she should consider selling her house. Depressed market or not, she didn't need this much space. Besides that, the neighborhood seemed to be spiraling downward steadily. Perhaps this was related to tenants like Jack Jones, or simply the fact that people were stretched too thin these days, and as a result, home maintenance chores got neglected. Whatever the case, there seemed to be a noticeable decline in neighborhood morale and general friendliness.

It didn't help matters that both her middle-aged children, Susan and Gary, lived hundreds of miles away. They were busy with their own lives, careers, and families and consequently rarely visited anymore. These days they preferred to send her airline tickets to come and spend time with them. But every time she went away, she felt a bit more concerned about leaving her home unattended— and with Jack Jones on the other side of the fence, she would worry even more now. Perhaps she should cancel her visit to Susan's next month. She usually spent most of January down there in the warm Florida sun, but who knew what kind of stunts that crazy neighbor might pull in her absence? And who would call her to let her know if anything was amiss? There could be a fire or a burglary or vandalism, and she probably wouldn't hear about it until she returned. A sad state of affairs indeed.

The shrill sound of the teakettle's whistle made her jump, and she knocked her favorite porcelain tea mug off the counter, where it promptly shattered into pieces on the faded yellow linoleum floor. "Oh, bother!" She turned off the stove, then went to fetch the broom and dustpan and clean up her mess. She had never been this edgy before—at least not before Jack Jones had moved into the neighborhood. And she was supposed to love her neighbor?

Chapter Two

Betty opened an Earl Grey teabag and dropped it in a porcelain mug that was still in one piece. As she poured the steaming water over it, she just shook her head. "Love your neighbor, bah humbug," she muttered as she went to the dining room. This was the spot where she normally enjoyed her afternoon cup of tea and looked out into her yard as the afternoon light came through the branches of the old maple tree. But she had barely sat down by the sliding glass door when she glimpsed a streak of blackish fur darting across her backyard like a hairy little demon. She blinked, then stood to peer out the window. "What in tarnation?"

There, hoisting his leg next to her beloved dogwood tree, a tree she'd nurtured and babied for years in a shady corner of her yard, was a scruffy-looking blackish-brown dog. At least she thought it was a dog. But it was a very ugly dog and not one she'd seen in the neighborhood before, although she couldn't be certain that it was a stray. With each passing year, it became harder and harder to keep track of people and pets.

She opened the sliding door and stepped out. "Shoo, shoo!" she called out. The dog looked at her with startled eyes as he lowered his leg, but he didn't run. "Go away," she yelled, waving her arms to scare him out of her yard. "Go home, you bad dog!" She clapped her hands and stomped her feet, and she was just about to either give up or throw something (perhaps the stupid dog was deaf and *very* dumb) when he took off running. He made a beeline straight for the fallen-down fence, neatly squeezing beneath the gap where fence boards had broken off, and escaped into Jack Jones's yard—just like he lived there!

"Well, of course," she said as she shut the door, locked it, and pulled her drapes closed. She picked up her teacup and went into the living room. "A mongrel dog for a mongrel man. Why should that surprise me in the least?"

She sat down in her favorite rocker-recliner and pondered her situation. What could possibly be done? How could she manage to survive not merely her loutish neighbor but his nasty little dog as well? It almost seemed as if Jack had sent the dog her way just to torture her some more. If a person couldn't feel comfortable and at home in their own house, what was the point of staying? What was keeping her here?

It was as if the writing were on the wall—a day of reckoning. Betty knew what she would do. She would sell her house and move away. That was the only way out of this dilemma. She wondered why she hadn't considered this solution last summer, back when Jack had first taken occupancy in the Spencer home. Didn't houses sell better in the warmer months? But perhaps it didn't matter. Still, she wasn't sure it made much sense to put up a For Sale sign during the holidays. Who would be out house shopping with less than two weeks before Christmas?

"Christmas…" She sighed, then sipped her lukewarm tea. How could it possibly be that time of year again? And what did she need to do in preparation for it? Or perhaps she didn't need to do anything. Who would really care if she baked cookies or not? Who would even notice if she didn't get out her old decorations? Christmas seemed like much ado about nothing. Oh, she didn't think the birth of Christ was nothing. But all the hullabaloo and overspending and commercialism that seemed to come with the holiday these days… When had it gone from being a wholesome family celebration to a stressful, jam-packed holiday that left everyone totally exhausted and up to their eyeballs in debt when it was over and done?

Betty used to love Christmastime. She would begin planning for it long in advance. Even the year that Chuck had died suddenly and unexpectedly just two days after Thanksgiving, Betty had somehow mustered the strength to give her children a fairly merry Christmas. They'd been grade schoolers at the time and felt just as confused and bereaved as she had. Still, she had known it was up to her to put forth her best effort. And so, shortly after the funeral, Betty had worn a brave smile and climbed up the rickety ladder to hang colorful strings of Christmas lights on the eaves of the house, "just like Daddy used to do." And then she got and decorated a six-foot fir tree, baked some cookies, wrapped a few gifts…all for the sake of her children. Somehow they made it through Christmas that year. And the Christmases thereafter.

When her son Gary was old enough (and taller than Betty), he eagerly took over the task of hanging lights on the house. And Susan happily took over the trimming of the tree. Each year the three of them would gather in the kitchen to bake all sorts of goodies, and then they would deliver festive cookie platters to everyone in the neighborhood. It became an expected tradition. And always their threesome family was lovingly welcomed into neighbors' homes, often with hot cocoa and glad tidings.

But times had changed since then. Betty had taken cookie platters to only a couple of neighbors last year. And perhaps this year she would take none. What difference would it make?

Betty set her empty tea mug aside and leaned back in her recliner. She reached down to pull out the footrest and soon felt herself drifting to sleep. She wished that she, like Rip Van Winkle, could simply close her eyes and sleep, sleep, sleep. She'd be perfectly happy if she were able to sleep right through Christmas. And then January would come, and she would figure out a way to sell this house and get out of this neighborhood. She would escape that horrid Jack Jones as well as the ugly mutt that most likely intended to turn her backyard into a doggy dump site.

Chapter Three

A little before seven on Monday morning, Betty woke to the sound of someone trying to break into her house. At least that was what it sounded like to her. She got out of bed and pulled on her old chenille robe, then reached for the cordless phone as she shoved her feet into her slippers. Some people, like her friend Marsha, would've been scared to death by something like this, but Betty had lived alone for so many years that she'd long since given up panic attacks. Besides, they weren't good for one's blood pressure.

But the screen door banged again, and she knew that someone was definitely on her porch. And so she shuffled out of her bedroom and peered through the peephole on the front door. But try as she might, she saw no one. Then she heard a whimpering sound and knew that it was an animal. Perhaps a raccoon or a possum, which often wandered into the neighborhood. She knew it could be dangerous, so she cautiously opened the front door. She quickly reached out to hook the screen door firmly before she looked down to see that it wasn't a raccoon or possum. It was that scruffy dog again. Jack Jones's mongrel. The dog crouched down, whimpering, and despite Betty's bitter feelings toward her neighbor, she felt a tinge of pity for the poor, dirty animal. And Betty didn't even like dogs.

"Go home, you foolish thing," she said. "Go bother your owner."

The dog just whined.

Betty knelt down with the screen still between her and the dog. "Go home," she said again. "Shoo!"

But the dog didn't budge. And now Betty didn't know what to do. So she closed the door and just stood there. If she knew Jack's phone number, she would call him and complain. But she didn't. She suspected the dog was hungry and cold, but she had no intention of letting the mongrel into her house. He looked as if he'd been rolling in the mud, and she'd just cleaned her floors on Saturday. But perhaps it wouldn't hurt to feed him a bit. Who knew when Jack had last given him a meal?

She went to look in her refrigerator, trying to determine what a hungry dog might eat. Finally, she decided on lunch meat. She peeled off several slices of processed turkey, then cautiously unlocked and opened the screen door just wide enough for her hand to slip out and toss the slices onto the porch. The dog was on them in seconds.

Betty went to her bedroom and took her time getting dressed, hoping that Jack's mutt would be gone by the time she finished. Perhaps he would beg food from another neighbor. But when she went to check her porch, he was still there. So she went to the laundry room and found a piece of clothesline to use as a leash.

"I hope you're friendly," she said. She bent over, hoping to tie the cord to the mutt's collar. But the dog had no collar. Instead he had a piece of string tied tightly around his neck. What kind of cruel gesture was that? She broke the dirty string and fashioned a looser sort of collar from the clothesline cord, looping it around his neck. To her relief, the mutt didn't make it difficult, didn't growl, didn't pull away. He simply looked up at her with sad brown eyes.

She stepped down from the porch and said, "Come!" The dog obeyed, walking obediently beside her. "Well, at least Jack has taught you some obedience," she said as she headed down the footpath to the sidewalk. "I'm taking you home now." Then she turned and marched down the sidewalk toward Jack's house. But now she wasn't so sure. What if this *wasn't* Jack's dog?

"Hello, Betty," Katie Gilmore called out. She stepped away from where the school bus had just picked up her twin girls. "How are you today?"

Betty smiled. "I'm fine, thank you."

Katie frowned down at the dog, then lowered her voice. "Does that dog belong to, uh, Jack Jones?"

"That's what I assume," Betty said. "I saw him in Jack's backyard yesterday."

"Yes, I noticed him over there too." Katie looked uneasy. "I hadn't known Jack had a dog. I hope he's friendly."

"I'm sure there's a lot we don't know about Jack." Betty forced a wry smile as she looked down at the dog. "But the dog seems to be friendly enough."

Katie frowned at the animal. "Poor thing."

Betty suspected Katie meant "poor thing" in relation to having Jack Jones as an owner. Everyone knew that Katie's husband, Martin, had experienced a bit of go-around with Jack last summer. Quiet Martin Gilmore had walked over and politely asked Jack to turn down his music one day. But according to Penny Horton, who'd been home at the time, Martin had been answered with a raised power tool and some rough language.

"Are you taking the dog to Jack's house?" Katie glanced over her shoulder toward the shabby-looking house.

"Yes. And I intend to give him a piece of my mind too."

Katie's brows arched. "Oh…" Then she reached in her coat pocket and pulled out a cell phone. "Want me to stick around, just in case?"

Betty wanted to dismiss Katie's offer as unnecessary, but then reconsidered. "I suppose that's not a bad idea."

"He can be a little unpredictable," Katie said quietly. "That's the main reason I've been making sure the girls get safely on and off the school bus these days."

Betty nodded. "I see."

"I'll just wait here," Katie said. "I'll keep an eye on you while you return the dog." She shook her head. "It looks neglected…and like it needs a bath."

Betty thought that wasn't the only thing the dog needed, and she intended to say as much to Jack Jones. Naturally, she would control her temper, but she would also let him know that organizations like the Humane Society or ASPCA would not be the least bit impressed with Jack's dog-owner skills.

When she got to Jack's house and knocked on the door, no one answered. However, his pickup was still parked in the front yard, so she suspected he was home and knocked again, louder this time. But still no answer. Finally, she didn't know what to do, so she simply tied the makeshift leash to a rickety-looking porch railing and left.

"He didn't answer the door?" Katie asked when Betty rejoined her.

"No." Betty turned and scowled at Jack's house. "I've a mind to call the Humane Society."

"It seems cruel to leave the dog tied to the porch," Katie said.

Betty shrugged. "I don't know what else to do."

"Well, I can see Jack's porch from my house. I'll keep an eye on the dog, and if Jack doesn't come out and let the dog inside or care for it, I'll give you a call."

Betty wanted to protest this idea. After all, why should that dog be her concern or responsibility? But she knew that would sound heartless and mean, so she just thanked Katie.

"Martin and I just don't know what to do about him," Katie said as she walked Betty back to her house. "I'll admit we didn't get off on the best foot with him, but we've tried to be friendly since then, and he just shuts us down."

"I know," Betty said. "He shuts everyone down."

"Now Martin is talking about moving. He's worried about the girls. He even did one of those police checks on Jack—you know, where you go online to see if the person has a record for being a sexual predator."

Betty's eyes opened wide. "Did he discover anything?"

"No." Katie looked dismal. "But now Martin is worried that Jack Jones might not be his real name."

Betty nodded. "The thought crossed my mind too."

"So what do you do about something like this?" Katie's tone was desperate now. "Do you simply allow some nutcase to ruin your neighborhood and drive you out of your home? Do you just give in?"

Betty sighed as she paused in front of her house. "I don't know what to tell you, Katie. I wish I did. And even though I've lived in this neighborhood for nearly forty years, I really don't have any answers. The truth is, I'm considering moving myself."

Katie shook her head. "That's just not fair."

"Well, I'm getting old." Betty forced a weak smile. "My house and yard are a lot of work for me, and the winters are long. Really, it might be for the best."

"Maybe so. But I have to say that Jack Jones has put a real damper on the holidays for me. The girls' last day of school is Wednesday, and I told Martin that I'm thinking about taking them to my mother's for all of winter break. Martin wasn't happy about that. He still has to work and isn't looking forward to coming home to an empty house while we're gone. But I told him that I didn't look forward to two weeks of being home with the girls with someone like Jack next door."

"That's too bad."

"I'll say. It's too bad that we don't feel safe or comfortable in our home."

Betty just shook her head. What was this neighborhood coming to?

"Anyway, I'll let you know how it goes with that poor dog," Katie said. And then they said good-bye and went their separate ways.

Once inside her house, Betty decided to call her daughter. Susan had always been sensible, not to mention a strong Christian woman. Plus she was a family counselor with a practice in her home. Surely she would have some words of wisdom to share. Some sage advice for her poor old mother. Betty planned to explain the situation in a calm and controlled manner, but once they got past the perfunctory greetings, Betty simply blurted out her plan to sell her home as soon as possible.

"When did you think you'd list it?" Susan sounded a little concerned.

"I'd like to put up a sign right now. But it probably makes more sense to wait until after the New Year."

"So…in January?"

"Yes. I didn't think anyone would want to buy a house right before Christmas."

"But you're coming here in January."

"Yes, I know. I'll put my house up for sale and leave."

"But the market is so low right now, Mom."

"I don't care."

"And I'll bet you haven't fixed anything up, have you?"

"I'll sell it as is."

"Yes…you could do that."

But Betty could hear the doubtful tone in Susan's voice growing stronger. "You think it's a bad idea, don't you?"

"I don't think it's a bad idea to sell your house. But I suppose I'm just questioning your timing. January isn't a good time to sell a house. The market is low right now. And I know you have some deferred maintenance issues to deal with and—"

"You think I should wait?"

"I think waiting until summer would be smarter."

"Oh."

"Why are you in this sudden rush, Mom?"

Betty felt silly now. To admit that it was her rude neighbor sounded so childish. And yet it was the truth. So she spilled the whole story, clear down to the scratch on her car, the broken tea mug, and the dirty dog.

Susan actually laughed.

"It is *not* funny."

"I'm sorry, Mom. I'm sure it's not funny to you. But hearing you tell it, well…" She chortled again. "It is kind of humorous."

"Humph."

"What kind of a dog was it?"

"What *kind* of a dog?" Betty frowned. "Good grief, how would I know? It was a mutt, a mongrel, a filthy dog that I would never allow inside my house. I can only imagine what Jack Jones's house must look like inside. It's a dump site outside. Did you know that there is a pink toilet in his backyard right this moment?" Betty went on to tell her daughter that Katie Gilmore was considering evacuating for Christmas and that Martin had actually done a criminal check on Jack.

"Oh dear," Susan said. "Do you think he's dangerous?"

"I don't know about that, but I do know he's very rude and inconsiderate and strange. I can only imagine what he's doing to the Spencer house. For all I know, he might even be a squatter or an escapee from the nut hatch, hiding out until the men in white coats show up to cart him away."

"Seriously?"

"Oh, I don't know."

"Have you even given him a chance, Mom? Maybe he's just lonely."

"Of course he's lonely. He pushes everyone away from him."

"But it sounds as if everyone is being confrontational."

"He invites confrontation!"

"Have you tried being kind to him?"

Betty didn't answer.

"I remember how we used to take cookies to our neighbors…"

Betty laughed now, but it was edged with bitterness. "I do not think Jack Jones would appreciate cookies, Susan. You don't understand the situation at all."

"Maybe not. But I do remember that my mother once told me that kindness builds bridges."

"All I want to build is a tall brick wall between Jack's house and mine." Betty mentioned the falling-down fence and disputed property line.

"See, that's just one more reason why it's not time to sell right now, Mom. You need to resolve those issues first."

"Maybe so."

Then Susan changed the subject by talking about the grandsons. Seth was still on a church missions trip, where they were putting in wells and septic systems in Africa.

"He just loves what he's doing there," Susan said, "and he loves the people. In fact, he's extended his stay until March now."

"And what about Marcus?" Betty asked. "How's school?"

"School is going fine. I think this is finals week. And, oh yeah, he has a girlfriend."

"A girlfriend? Have you met her?"

"No. But it sounds like he may be going to her house for Christmas."

"So you and Tim will be alone for Christmas?" Betty had booked her flight to Florida months ago, but now she considered changing the dates so that she could be with her daughter during the holidays too. Why hadn't she thought of that sooner? Oh yes, she remembered—her commitment to help with the Deerwood anniversary party just days before Christmas.

"Not exactly alone…" Susan explained how Tim had put together a plan to share the expenses of a small yacht with some other couples while they toured the Florida Keys together during the holidays.

"That sounds like fun." Betty frowned out

the back window. Jack's dog was in her back-yard again!

"I wasn't sure at first, but I'm getting excited now."

"Well, I'm excited too," Betty said in an angry voice. "That mongrel dog has sneaked into my backyard again!" The mutt was making a doggy deposit right next to her beloved dogwood tree! Did the mongrel think that because it was a *dog*wood tree, it was open season for dogs? "That horrible animal! I think I'll take a broom to him."

"Oh, Mom!" Susan sounded disappointed. "That's so mean. You've never been mean like that before."

"Are you suggesting it's not mean for Jack to force me to clean up after his dog? To remove nasty dog piles from my own backyard?"

"That's not the dog's fault, Mom. You said yourself that the fence is falling apart. What do you expect?"

"I expect the owner to take some responsibility for his animal. Maybe I should go throw something at the nasty dog."

"What happened to the sweet Christian woman I used to know?" Susan asked.

"Jack Jones is making her lose her mind."

"Oh, Mother, you can do better than that. Remember what you used to tell me when I was young and I'd get so angry that I'd feel like killing someone?"

"What?" Betty felt a headache coming on.

"You'd say, 'Why don't you kill them with kindness, Susan?'"

Betty rubbed her forehead as she remembered her own words.

"So, why don't you do that now, Mom? Why don't you kill Jack Jones with kindness?"

"And his little dog too?"

"Yes. And his little dog too."

Betty promised her daughter that she'd consider the challenge, and she was just about to say good-bye when Susan said quickly, "Hey, I almost forgot to tell you."

"What's that?"

"Have you heard from Gary lately?"

Suddenly Betty felt worried. She could tell by Susan's voice that something was wrong. Surely no harm had come to her son. "No...I haven't spoken to him since Thanksgiving. Is everything okay?"

"Well, I wasn't supposed to say anything to you..."

"Anything about what?" Betty was really concerned now.

"It's Avery."

"Oh." Avery was Gary's stepdaughter. She was in her mid-twenties and still acted like an adolescent. "What's happened with Avery?"

"She's gone missing."

"Missing?"

"Gary called awhile back and told me they haven't heard from her since October."

"October?" Betty considered this. "Gary didn't mention this when he called me at Thanksgiving."

"He probably didn't want to worry you."

"I see."

"But they're starting to get concerned. I mean, Avery's been known to take off and do some irresponsible things before, but not for this long. And she usually checks in from time to time."

"And she hasn't checked in?"

"No." Susan sighed. "Apparently Avery got into a big fight with Stephanie."

Stephanie was Avery's mom, Gary's second wife. She was an intelligent woman and very beautiful, but her temper was a little volatile, and this sometimes worried Betty. "When was the fight?" Betty asked.

"Mid-October."

"Naturally, Avery's been missing since then?"

"Pretty much so."

"Oh dear, that's quite a while. I hope she's okay."

"I'm sure she's fine. Avery probably just wants to teach her mom a lesson. Anyway, I've really been praying for her, and I thought you might want to also."

"Yes, of course I'll be praying for her."

"And I'll assume you're praying for your neighbor too?" Susan's voice sounded a tiny bit sarcastic now.

"I'm *trying* to pray for him," Betty said. "But it's not easy."

"Well, I'll start praying for him too, Mom. Keep me posted."

"And you keep me posted on Avery."

"Sure, just don't let Gary know that I mentioned it. And in the meantime, remember what I told you."

"What's that?" Now Betty felt confused. They'd talked of so much—to sell or not to sell the house, Avery's disappearance.

"You know, take your own advice—kill him with kindness."

Betty looked out at her backyard only to

see that the stupid dog was now digging in her favorite tulip bed. "I'll kill him, all right," she snapped.

"Mom!"

"Yes, yes, like you said, with kindness. I have to go now, dear." But after she hung up and went outside, Betty did not have kindness in her heart. And when she saw that someone—and it could only be Jack—had hammered a board over the opening in the fence, on his side of the fence, she felt outraged. Had he allowed his dog to pass through and then sealed off the doggy escape route? What was wrong with that man?

She marched out to the woodshed and got an old ax. The dog followed her, watching as she took the ax to the fence and chopped an even bigger hole. Fortunately, the fence was so rotten that it wasn't much of a challenge. The challenge came with getting the dumb dog to pass back through the hole onto his own side of the fence. She went back to the house and utilized another piece of lunch meat to entice the mutt into Jack's yard. Once he was there, she shoved several pieces of firewood in the hole to block the new opening of the fence.

She let out a tired sigh as she looked across

the sagging and now somewhat ravaged-look-
ing fence. The dog just sat there in the yard
and looked at her with those sad brown eyes.

"I'm sorry," she said. "Dogs don't get to
pick their masters, just like I don't get to pick
my neighbors. We both need to make the best
of it."

But as she walked away, she felt guilty on
several levels. And the expression on the poor
mutt's face seemed to be imprinted in her
mind. When had she become so mean?

Chapter Four

Betty finally had to pull the drapes on the windows that faced her backyard because she could still see the dog sitting out there in the bitter cold just staring toward her house in the most pitiful way. She picked up the phone and considered calling information for the number of the Humane Society. Why shouldn't she turn Jack Jones in for dog neglect? He deserved it. But then she remembered her daughter's words. And so she replaced the phone and decided to go to the grocery store instead.

With Susan's challenge running through her mind, Betty decided she would give this her best attempt. She would do all she could to "kill Jack and his dog with kindness." And, although she normally lived on a fairly frugal grocery budget, today she would throw caution to the wind. So, along with her normal groceries, Betty also gathered up the ingredients for cookies and fudge. After that she stopped in the pet aisle, where she added to her shopping cart a red nylon collar and matching leash, some dog shampoo, a couple of cans of dog food, and even a red and green plaid bed.

"Looks like somebody is getting a dog for Christmas." The cashier winked at her as he bagged up her purchases.

"Looks that way, doesn't it?"

"Or maybe the family pooch is getting something from Santa?" he asked.

She just gave him a stiff smile and paid in cash from her envelope. This was a habit she'd developed years ago when the children still lived at home. But today's shopping had used up the remainder of her December grocery budget. The month was only half over, and she usually went shopping once a week. But perhaps it would be worth it. Perhaps this was how she would buy peace. And, if the kindness plan didn't work, she would simply sell her house, and she might even toss budgeting out the window. Maybe she'd do like

Susan—board a boat and just sail away into the sunset. Why not?

But as Betty loaded her unusual purchases into her car, trying to ignore the J-shaped gash on the front right fender, she felt rather foolish. What on earth was she doing with this doggy paraphernalia anyway? As she closed her trunk, she feared she might be getting senile. Or maybe she had simply lost her mind. Had Jack Jones driven her mad?

To distract herself from Jack, she focused her attention on praying for Avery. Although they weren't related by blood, Avery had started calling Betty "Grandma" shortly after her mother married Betty's son Gary a dozen years ago. And Betty had adopted Avery into her heart as a granddaughter.

Betty remembered the first time she'd met the quiet, preadolescent girl. It had been shortly before the wedding, and Betty had suspected that Avery wasn't too pleased with her mother's marriage. But during the reception, Betty and Avery seemed to bond, which was a good thing since Betty was to keep Avery while Gary and Stephanie honeymooned in the Caribbean. Naturally, Avery had been reluctant to be away from her friends, and Betty had been a bit apprehensive about caring for a girl she barely knew, but by the end of the two weeks, they'd become fast friends. Avery had even cried when it was time to go home.

Over the following few years, Avery usually spent at least two weeks of her summer vacation at Betty's home. And sometimes spring break as well. But everything seemed to change when Avery turned sixteen. That was when, according to Betty's son, Avery became a "wild child." And Gary worried that his stepdaughter's strong will would be too much for his aging mother. Just the same, Betty missed those visits, and over the years she continued to send Avery cards and gifts, and occasionally money, for birthdays, holidays, and graduation. Betty seldom got a thank-you in return, but she figured young people weren't trained in the social graces very much these days.

As Betty pulled into her driveway, then carefully parked her car in the garage again, her thoughts returned to Jack Jones. Suddenly she wondered just how she planned to present her eccentric "gifts" to her neighbor. More than that, she wondered how he would receive them. Besides being rude and inconsiderate and painfully private, Jack Jones struck her as being an extremely proud young man, and stubborn too. For all she knew, he might throw her silly purchases right back in her face. Really, it was a crazy idea—what had she been thinking? Perhaps the best plan would be to simply forget the whole thing and take the items back tomorrow. Even if the store refused to refund her money, they could probably give her a credit. And so she carried her groceries into the house but left the doggy items in her car to be returned later.

Still feeling a bit silly, she stowed her groceries away—all except for the baking ingredients, which she lined up on the counter by the stove, just like she used to do before a full day of holiday baking. Then she stood there staring at the bags of chocolate chips, nuts, dried fruits, and powdered and brown sugar, and finally just shook her head. Had she lost her mind?

Did she really plan on making Christmas goodies to give to her neighbors—people she barely knew? And to share her homemade treats with the likes of Jack Jones? Was that even sensible? What if she were setting herself up for trouble? What if Jack Jones was a dangerous man? A criminal? It was one thing to love her neighbor, but what if her neighbor was a murderer, or a pedophile, or a sociopath? Should she take cookies to a man like that?

With a little more than a week still left until Christmas, she decided to think about these things later. Right now she was too tired to think clearly, let alone bake cookies.

Betty awoke to the sound of something knocking on the front door. She blinked and slowly pushed herself out of her recliner, thinking it must be that mongrel dog again. Why wouldn't he just leave her alone? Didn't he know where he lived? She groaned as she made her way through the living room. Her arthritis was acting up, probably as a result of this cold, damp weather.

But when she looked through the peephole, not expecting to see anyone, she saw what appeared to be an attractive, dark-haired young woman. A scarlet-red scarf was wound so high up her neck that it concealed the lower half of her face, so it was hard to tell who it was. Feeling slightly befuddled and not completely awake, Betty just stared at the person, thinking to herself that those dark brown eyes looked oddly familiar.

"Avery!" Betty fumbled with the deadbolt

and opened the door so she could unlock and open the screen door. "Avery!" she cried again as she embraced the girl in a warm hug and pulled her into the house. "I almost didn't recognize you. It's been so long."

As Betty closed the front door and relocked the deadbolt, Avery began to unwind the scarf from around her neck. "Hi, Grandma," she said in a tired voice. "Sorry to bust in on you like this, but I was, uh, in the neighborhood…"

"I'm glad you came! I'm so happy to see you." Betty took the girl's slightly damp parka and hung it on the hall tree to dry out, along with the snagged-up scarf that appeared to be nearly six feet long. "How are you?"

"Oh, I'm okay…I guess." Avery pushed some loose strands of dark hair away from her face. The rest of her hair was pulled back into a long and messy ponytail. Her skin seemed pale, there were dark smudges under her eyes, and without her parka, she seemed very thin and waiflike.

"Come in and sit down and get warm." Betty motioned Avery toward the living room.

"Wow, everything looks just the same, Grandma." Avery looked around the room with hungry eyes. "Nothing has changed."

Betty laughed. "I guess that's how it is when we get old. We're comforted by keeping things the same."

"I'm comforted too." Avery sat on the couch and picked up a pillow with a crocheted covering that Betty's mother had made for her years ago. Avery just stared at the pattern of colors—roses, lilacs, and periwinkle. "I always loved this pillow, Grandma."

Betty smiled. "I'll make sure to leave it to you in my will."

Now Avery looked sad as she set the pillow aside. "Don't say that. I'd hate to think of you dying. I don't want the pillow that bad."

"Don't worry, I don't plan on going anytime soon."

Avery nodded. "Good."

"So, what brings you into my neck of the woods?"

Avery sighed. "I don't know…"

Betty considered the situation. She didn't want to press too hard, didn't want to make Avery so uncomfortable that she'd be tempted to run off again. Better just to keep things light. "Say, are you hungry?"

Avery looked up with eager eyes. "Yes! I'm starving."

"Well, I just went to the grocery store

today. And I haven't had lunch yet either. Why don't we see what we can find?"

Before long, Betty had grilled cheese sandwiches cooking on one burner, and Avery was stirring cream of tomato soup on another.

"This feels good," Avery said.

"Cooking?"

"Yes. Being in a real kitchen, smelling food…it feels kinda homey."

Betty had noticed how grimy Avery's hands and nails looked. Like she hadn't bathed in days, maybe even weeks. "Well, everything's about ready," she told her. "Maybe you'd like to go wash up before we eat."

Avery nodded. "Yeah, that's a good idea."

Soon they were both sitting at the kitchen table, and, as usual, Betty bowed her head to say grace.

"Just like always," Avery said after Betty finished. "You still thank God every time you eat?"

"I try to."

"That's nice." Avery smiled and took a big bite of her sandwich, then another, and then, in no time, her sandwich was gone and she was shoveling down her soup.

"I'll bet you could eat another sandwich," Betty said.

"Do you mind?"

"Not at all." Betty got up to fix another.

"Grandma?"

"Yes?" Betty paused from slicing the cheese.

"Why is it so dark in here? Why are the curtains all shut?"

"Oh." Betty frowned. "It's a long story."

"I've got time."

So, as Betty grilled the second sandwich, she began to explain about her unpredictable and somewhat thoughtless neighbor. She tried not to paint too horrible a picture of him. After all, she didn't want to frighten Avery. But she did want her to understand that the man was a bit of a loose cannon. "And now that he's got this crazy dog, well, it's getting to be even more complicated."

"What kind of a dog?"

"Who knows? A mutt."

Avery laughed. "Oh."

Betty reached over to open the drapes that had been blocking the view of the backyard. But to her pleasant surprise, the dog was not anywhere in sight. "Hopefully, Jack has enough sense to put his dog inside," she said. "Because it looks like it's about to rain again. And as cold as it is out there, I expect it might turn into a freezing rain by tonight."

Avery stood and began to clear the table. "I'll clean these things up."

"Thank you," Betty said. "I appreciate that."

"You go put your feet up," Avery said. "Leave everything to me."

"Now that's an offer I cannot refuse."

For the second time that day, Betty got into her recliner and put her feet up and was about to doze off when she heard something at the door. Avery was still in the kitchen, so Betty slowly made her way out of her chair, went to the door, and realized that this time it really was that dog again. In Betty's excitement over seeing Avery, she'd forgotten to lock the screen door, and now the dog had wedged itself between the loose screen door and the front door, almost as if he thought it was a place to seek shelter. Betty had barely opened the door and was about to shoo it away, but the dog shot between her legs and right into the house.

"No! No!" Betty waved her hands. "Out of my house, you mongrel! Get out of here! Get out! Get out!" But the dog ran down the hallway and headed back toward the bedrooms.

"What?" Avery came out holding a sudsy saucepan. "Do you want me to leave?"

"No, not you. That darn dog sneaked into my house. I was yelling at it to go away."

"Oh, I thought you meant me."

"No, of course not." Betty pointed down the hallway. "He went that way. Help me catch him."

They finally cornered the runaway dog in the bathroom, where it cowered on Betty's pale pink bath mat. Or what used to be pale pink before being spotted with muddy smudges.

"Bad dog!" Betty shouted.

But Avery knelt down beside the dog, holding its head in her hands and looking into its face. "Poor thing. Look how dirty and cold it is."

"Yes, Jack Jones is a very bad man. He should be arrested for pet neglect, among other things."

"Can I give him a bath?" Avery asked with hopeful eyes.

"A *bath*?" Betty gasped. "You mean right here in my bathtub?"

Avery nodded.

Betty wrung her hands. "But he's filthy. It will be such a mess, the whole bathroom will smell like a dog."

"I'll clean everything up when I'm done."

Avery looked sad now. "Look, he's so cold... he's shivering." She touched his muddy brown coat. "And he's so dirty and matted and sad. Please, Grandma, we can't let him go back like this."

Betty got an idea. "Okay, you can bathe him, but not in here. You can put him in the laundry sink. That won't be such a mess."

"Okay!" Avery scooped up the dirt-encrusted dog and carried him through the house with Betty trailing behind her, carrying the half-washed saucepan in one hand and the soiled bath mat in the other. Betty deposited these items, then dug through her linen closet to find two old towels to give to Avery. By now the laundry sink was nearly full.

"Do you have any soap to use on him?" Avery asked.

Betty remembered her recent doggy purchases. "As a matter of fact, I have just the thing." She headed out to the garage to get the shampoo and returned with all the doggy items in tow.

Avery's eyes grew wide. "Where did you get all that stuff?"

"At the store."

"For *this* dog?"

"I wanted to be a good neighbor." Now

Betty felt a little sheepish to admit this, since she'd just tried to chase the mutt out of her house. "I thought Jack Jones needed some help with his dog."

"I'll say." Avery reached for the bottle of shampoo and began to lather up the wet dog. "I have a feeling this is going to take awhile."

"I'll leave you to it," Betty said. She went to finish up the nearly cleaned kitchen, then on to the hallway and bathroom to mop up the dirt the dog had tracked in, and finally back to her recliner, where she collapsed in exhaustion and closed her eyes.

When Betty opened her eyes about an hour later, she saw a clean brown dog lying in the plaid bed, wearing a red collar and snoozing comfortably. But where was Avery? Surely she hadn't left. Not in this weather. And not after dark. Betty went down the hallway and noticed the bathroom door was shut with a light coming from beneath it, and she could hear water running. Avery had probably discovered that after bathing the filthy dog, she needed a bath as well. Hopefully, this meant she planned to stay awhile.

And if Betty had her way, Avery would at least spend the night here. Not that she could force her to stay longer than that. But

Betty would certainly put her foot down if Avery made any attempt to leave this evening. And so Betty went to check on the guest room, the same room Avery had inhabited so many years before. She turned the baseboard heater up, fluffed the pillows, and added an extra quilt at the end of the bed. Avery hadn't brought any luggage with her, nothing besides an oversized bag. Was it possible she had only the clothes on her back? And if so, why?

Betty went to her own room and retrieved a pair of pretty pink pajamas that Susan had given her last Christmas. She'd never even worn them. Not because she didn't like them, but probably because she'd been saving them. But saving them for what? Well, she didn't know. It's just the way she was about some things. Perhaps she'd been saving them for Avery. Whatever the reason, she neatly refolded them and placed them by Avery's pillow. Then she turned on the small light on the bedside table and smiled in satisfaction. Very welcoming.

"I hope you don't mind that I took a shower," Avery said when she emerged from the bathroom with wet hair. "But I was kind of a mess."

"You did a good job of cleaning up that

dog." Betty nodded to where the mutt was still sleeping. Then she frowned at Avery's soiled T-shirt and jeans. "But why did you put on your dirty clothes again?"

"Because they're all I have."

"You don't have any other clothes?"

Avery just shrugged. "I'll be okay."

Betty shook her head. "No, you will not be okay, Avery. I know you're smaller than I am, at least around, and I think you might be a bit taller. But I might have something for you to wear while we wash your clothes."

"Okay." Avery smiled.

"And the guest room is all ready for you. In fact, if you like you can simply put on the pajamas I laid out for you."

"Okay," Avery said again.

"And then we'll sit down and talk."

Avery bent down to pat the dog, and he looked up with what almost seemed a grateful expression.

"He looks like he's got some terrier in him," Betty said.

"Yeah, that's what I thought too."

"Well, I need to figure out how to get him back to Jack now."

Avery frowned. "I don't think that horrible Jack person deserves to own this dog.

He's got a really sweet disposition, and Jack sounds like a total monster. The poor dog's hair was so matted and filthy that it took a bunch of shampooing and rinsing to get him clean. And the whole time he was totally patient. I could tell he liked the attention. But I could feel his ribs. I think he hasn't been fed properly."

Betty nodded. "I'm sure you're right about Jack not being a fit pet owner, but I don't know what we should do about it."

"We should report him to the ASPCA."

"That thought has crossed my mind." Betty pressed her lips together firmly. She wondered what kind of a Christian witness it would be for her to turn in her neighbor. On the other hand, what kind of a Christian allows an innocent animal to suffer that kind of neglect?

She looked at Avery's dripping hair and dirty clothes. "We'll figure out the doggy dilemma later. In the meantime, why don't you change out of those dirty things and get your hair dried before you catch pneumonia."

Avery patted the dog one more time, then left the room. Betty sighed loudly as she sat back down in her recliner. Rocking back and forth, she pondered over what should be done—not so much about the dog as about her wayward granddaughter. Why had Avery shown up like this? And where had she been these past months? Should Betty call Avery's parents? Or should she simply encourage Avery to let them know she was okay?

Betty looked over to where the dog was sleeping again. What was her responsibility for that poor dog? Avery was probably right, he did seem like a nice dog. Not that Betty wanted or needed a dog—she most definitely did not!

And then there was Jack to consider. Betty leaned her head back and closed her eyes. Only yesterday, her biggest challenge was to stop envying her friend's new coat and to make an attempt to love her unlovable neighbor. But her problems seemed to have multiplied. Now she had not only Jack to contend with but a neglected dog and a troubled granddaughter as well. Oh my!

Chapter Five

"It will serve him right," Avery said. They had just agreed to keep Jack's dog overnight. Perhaps he'd be worried about his animal and want to take better care of him. Or so they hoped.

"And when I return the dog to him tomorrow morning, I'll warn Jack that this neglect cannot continue." Betty stirred the simmering rolled oats, relieved that Avery didn't mind having oatmeal for dinner. It was one of Betty's favorites.

"Tell Jack that you'll report him if he doesn't treat his dog right," Avery said.

Betty nodded. "I'll try to make that clear. But I don't want to be too confrontational with him."

"Why not? He's a total jerk, Grandma."

"Yes, he is a jerk. But he's also my neighbor. And the Bible teaches us to love our neighbors." Betty turned off the stove and removed the pan.

"Even when they're jerks?"

"Even when they're jerks, and even if they're our worst enemies."

"That doesn't sound possible."

Betty smiled. "Yes, I've felt like that myself. It's a challenge."

Avery was studying the calendar that was taped to Betty's fridge. "Wow, is this what day it is?"

Betty looked to where Avery's finger was pointing and nodded. "That's right."

"It's like eight days until Christmas."

Betty spooned out the oatmeal and set the bowls on the kitchen table. She'd already put out brown sugar, raisins, walnuts, and milk to go with it. "I can hardly believe it myself," she said as she sat down.

"Whose fiftieth anniversary is this?" Avery asked as she continued to study the calendar.

"My good friends Marsha and Jim Deerwood."

"Oh, I thought maybe it was yours." Avery kind of laughed and joined Betty at the Formica-topped table. "But I guess you don't celebrate anniversaries if you're not both around."

"To be honest, I do." Betty bowed her head and said a quick blessing over their oatmeal. When she looked up, Avery had a curious expression.

"You celebrate your anniversary?"

"I know it sounds silly. In fact, I've never told anyone before. But yes, I do. I fix a special little dinner, set the table for two, and think about Chuck, and I remember our wedding day."

"What day did you get married?"

"June 20. Last summer would've been our fiftieth anniversary."

"Wow. That's a long time."

Betty nodded as she chewed a bite.

"Why didn't you ever remarry?"

Betty considered this. It was a question she used to get asked a lot. But not so much as the years piled on. "I just never met the right man. It was hard to measure up to Chuck."

"But don't you get lonely?"

"I suppose…a little. Especially after I retired from the electric company. But I've had plenty of time to get used to being alone. Also I have my church, my friends, my neighbors."

"Some of your neighbors sound awful."

Betty forced a smile. "The neighborhood has changed over the years."

"So, are you going anywhere for Christmas?" Avery asked.

"No. I plan to stay home this year." Betty poured more milk on her oatmeal. "I offered to help with my friends' fiftieth anniversary, and it's just a few days before Christmas. Then I'm scheduled to go to Susan's shortly after the New Year."

"Oh."

"What about you, Avery? Do you have special plans for the holidays?"

Avery stirred her oatmeal without looking up.

"I know that you had a fight with your mother."

"Did they call you?"

"No…" Betty wasn't sure how much she should press Avery.

"Well, I guess I'm kind of like Jack's dog."

"How's that?"

"If you don't treat me right, I run away."

Betty chuckled.

"Do you know how many times my mom's been married?"

"I thought Gary was her second husband."

"That's what she *wanted* you to think."

"So, he's not?"

"Nope. She was married *three times* before Gary. He's her fourth."

Betty tried not to look too surprised.

"Gary knows about it now."

"But he didn't before?"

"Nope."

Betty wondered how Gary had reacted to this news but didn't want to ask.

"And I'm the one who told him."

Betty lifted her brows. "And how did your mother feel about that?"

"That's what started our big fight. Actually, the fight was already in motion, but that's what made it really take off. Mom told me to leave and never come back."

"Your mother said that?"

"Pretty much so."

"But she was probably speaking out of her emotions, Avery. I doubt that she really meant it."

Avery shrugged as she stuck her spoon back in her bowl. "I think she meant it."

Now Betty didn't know what to say. Really, what could she say? It wasn't as if this was her business. And she'd heard enough about Avery's adolescence to know there were probably two sides to this story. Still, Betty felt disappointed that Stephanie had deceived her as well as her son. She really was curious as to how Gary had reacted to this bit of news. She knew Gary loved Stephanie. But she also knew he had a strong sense of propriety. He would not like discovering he'd been lied to.

"Anyway," Avery continued, "I do not plan to be home for the holidays. I doubt that I'd even be welcome there."

"You're welcome to stay with me."

Avery brightened. "Thanks!"

"But on one condition."

Now she frowned slightly. "What?"

"Let your parents know where you are."

Avery seemed to be thinking about this.

"I realize you're not a child, Avery. How old are you now, anyway?"

"I turned twenty-three in September."

Betty shook her head. "And I completely forgot to send you a card."

"That's okay."

"But as I was saying, you're not a child. You're an adult, but that means you need to be responsible. And a responsible adult lets family members know that she's okay."

"Yeah, you're probably right."

"So if you take care of that, you're welcome to stay here during the holidays."

Avery nodded.

Betty wasn't sure what more she should say to the girl. She certainly had questions, but she didn't want to make Avery feel like she was participating in the Spanish Inquisition tonight. Nor did she want to lecture her or drive her away. Betty suspected that Avery was broke. And it appeared that she had nothing more than what was on her back and in the oversized bag she'd tossed into the guest room.

Betty knew enough about Avery's past to know that, much to her parents' dismay, she'd dropped out of college at the end of her junior year. Avery had claimed that a degree would not guarantee a job. But since leaving school, her employment history had been splotchy at best. According to Susan—Betty's best news source since Gary preferred to keep his mother in the dark—Avery had held a variety of low-paying and unimpressive jobs. And she seemed to bounce back and forth between living at home and staying with friends. Now she was here.

But the truth was, Betty was grateful for the company. And she didn't mind that Avery would be with her through the holidays. Just as long as she informed her parents of her whereabouts. Betty did not want to find herself in the center of a family feud.

Betty glanced at the kitchen clock to see that it was past seven. "I suppose you should wait to call your parents until tomorrow since it's pretty late where they live."

Avery looked relieved. "Yeah. I'll call in the morning."

Just then the dog wandered into the kitchen, going straight to Avery as if they were old friends. "I think we should set the dog's bed and things up in the laundry room," Betty said.

"Is it okay if I feed him again?" Avery asked. "He seemed pretty hungry."

"I'll leave that up to you. Just make sure he has a chance to go out and do his business before you tell him good night."

Betty awoke to a high-pitched whining the next morning. It took her a moment to figure out that the sound was coming from the laundry room, more specifically from the dog. And then she realized that the dog needed to go outside for a potty break. She let him out into the backyard and watched from the open doorway as the dog started to hike up his leg on the trunk of the dogwood tree again.

"No, no!" Betty yelled from where she was standing in the house. The dog looked at her but didn't seem to understand. She just shook her head, tightened the belt of her robe, and waited for him to finish his business.

Betty let the dog back in through the sliding door. "Don't get too comfortable here," she warned as she attempted to usher him back to the laundry room. But since he didn't seem very eager to go, she resorted to using an opened can of dog food to entice him. Holding it in front of his nose, she led him into the room.

"Now, as bad as your master may be, he's still your owner." Betty spooned some food into the bowl. "And like it or not, you're going back to him today."

Betty went to check on Avery, only to discover that she was still sound asleep. Probably exhausted from her travels or whatever it was she'd been doing. Betty decided to just let the girl rest. Besides, it might make it easier to return the dog without Avery around to stir things up.

Betty knew that Avery was outraged by Jack's attitude toward his dog. Perhaps it had to do with Avery's feelings about how her mother was treating her. Or maybe it was just empathy. Whatever the case, Betty knew this was something she should handle on her own. So she gathered up the dog things and put them in an oversized trash bag, then leashed up the dog and proceeded down the street and around the corner toward Jack's house.

As usual, his pickup was parked diagonally across the front yard, and the place still looked like a wreck. And just like yesterday, no one answered when she rang the doorbell. Then it occurred to her that the doorbell, like the rest of the house, could be out of order. And so she knocked loudly. But as she knocked, she noticed that the door was ajar. She pushed it open slightly and was tempted to peek inside, but she worried that she might be caught and accused of trespassing, so she controlled herself. Instead, she simply unlatched the leash from the little dog's collar and shoved the unsuspecting pooch through the open door, then closed it firmly. She left the leash and the bag of doggy things on the front porch. Resisting the urge to brush off her hands or shake the dust off her feet, Betty turned and marched away. Mission accomplished.

Betty went home and cleaned up the laundry room, trying to eradicate the damp doggy odor that seemed to permeate the tight area. She put in a load of laundry, including Avery's soiled clothes and the smelly dog towels, and then she straightened the house and gave the kitchen a good scrub down.

Eventually she went to check on Avery again. It was nearly eleven, and the girl was still fast asleep. But Betty remembered the dark circles she'd noticed beneath Avery's eyes last night. She probably needed a good rest. And Betty needed to put her feet up. But first she called Susan. When she got Susan's answering service, she left a message, explaining that Avery was safe and with her, and that she'd make sure Avery called Gary and Stephanie as soon as possible.

It was almost one by the time Avery made an appearance. By then Betty had enjoyed a short nap and come up with a plan for their day. She explained her idea to Avery as she set a peanut butter and jelly sandwich and glass of milk in front of her. That used to be Avery's favorite lunch, but that had been quite some time ago. She hoped it didn't look too childish now.

"I've got errands to run for my friends' anniversary party," Betty said as she refilled

Avery's milk glass. "And then I thought we'd take you shopping for some clothes."

"Cool." Avery's eyes lit up like she'd just won the lottery or an all-expense-paid shopping trip.

Betty cleared her throat. "But since I live on a pretty tight budget, I'm taking you to a thrift store to shop. In fact, Goodwill is located in the same strip mall as the party store where I need to shop. We'll save on gas money as well. I hope you don't mind second-hand clothing."

"That's okay," Avery said with her mouth full. "I like retro clothes."

"Retro?" Betty thought about this. "Well, that's a good thing."

"You're probably wondering where my other clothes are." Avery took a long swig of milk.

"Yes, I suppose I was."

As Avery devoured the second half of her sandwich, she told Betty a crazy story about traveling with a friend named Kendra. They ran out of money and panhandled until they could afford bus tickets to L.A., where they planned to stay with a friend for a while, but there was some kind of disturbance on the bus during the night.

"It was all this old dude's fault." Avery shook her head as she set her milk glass in the sink. "He was like forty, and he'd been coming on to both of us, so Kendra got fed up and smacked him in the nose." Avery made a face. "So this jerk made a big fuss, telling the driver that we were propositioning him, which was so not true, and the driver put Kendra and me off the bus, right out in the middle of nowhere. So we hitchhiked, and the guy who picked us up offered to buy us breakfast in this little town. We left our backpacks in his car, and while we were using the bathroom, he took off with our stuff."

"Oh my." Betty just shook her head. "You should be thankful he didn't hurt you girls. Hitchhiking sounds very dangerous."

"I guess. After that, Kendra and I got in a huge fight and went our separate ways. Since I wasn't too far from your place, I caught a ride into town…and now here I am." She smiled. "I was so glad to see they still hang those candy cane decorations on the streetlights here. So old-fashioned and sweet."

Betty nodded. "Yes, that's one way to look

at it. Some people just think it's because the city is cheap." She pointed to Avery's dirty dishes in the clean sink. "I'd appreciate it if you picked up after yourself while you're here, Avery. The dishes in the dishwasher are dirty."

"Uh, sure, okay."

"Thank you." Betty watched as Avery rinsed the dishes and put them in the dishwasher. She didn't want to sound like an old curmudgeon. But she didn't want to encourage laziness in the girl either.

"No problem." Avery closed the dishwasher and turned to look at her. "Now what?"

"Your clothes should be clean and ready for you," Betty said. "I heard the dryer buzzer a few minutes ago."

"Thanks."

Betty glanced up at the clock. "And if you don't mind, I'd like to leave by two. I want to get back home before it starts to get dark. That's around four thirty these days."

"No problem."

As Avery got dressed, Betty went to fetch her coat and purse but was interrupted by a banging on the front door.

And there on the porch was that dog again!

"What on earth are you doing back here?"

she said. Naturally, the dog didn't answer, but his tail waved back and forth with canine enthusiasm. And there on a corner of her porch was the same garbage bag Betty had left at Jack's house. That's when Betty noticed a piece of paper taped on the dog's red collar. Stooping to examine it more closely, Betty saw some words scribbled in pencil: "Thanks, but NO thanks!"

She blinked and stood up. Well, it just figured. She must've insulted Jack Jones with her generosity. Fine, if he didn't want the doggy things, she didn't care. Why had she expected a normal reaction from the foolish young man in the first place? Still, it seemed irresponsible to send his dog like this to inform her. And it did seem a waste of money since she certainly couldn't return these used items to the store. Besides, it appeared obvious that Jack needed some help in the doggy department.

"Your owner doesn't have a lick of sense!" Betty frowned at the dog. His tail stopped wagging, and he looked somewhat confused by the tone of Betty's voice. "Oh, I'm not scolding you. It's just that your master is very stubborn." Betty thought for a moment. "But then, so am I."

Betty went into the house and dug out a small white index card, then wrote "Merry Christmas" in bold letters with a red felt pen. She stuck a hole in one corner and threaded a piece of yarn, then tied it securely around the dog's collar. "We'll see who wins this little battle of the wills."

She gathered up the bag containing the dog paraphernalia and threw it over one shoulder like a grumpy Santa. Taking the leash in her other hand, Betty marched back to Jack's house. His pickup was still there, but this time the door was firmly closed, and she could hear his power tools running inside. Just the same, she tried knocking on the door, then banging loudly, but to no avail. So she retrieved the plaid dog bed from the bag, shook it out, and set it on a protected corner of the porch. She tied the leash to the nearby post, leaving enough slack so the dog could move around a bit.

Betty did feel a bit sorry for leaving the dog like that, but it was better than him running loose in the neighborhood or being hit by a car. And she and Avery could check on his welfare when they returned from their shopping and errands in a couple of hours. Hopefully the dog would bark and make some

kind of fuss to get his owner's attention before long. Betty just hoped that Jack would
take the hint that the doggy goodies were intended to be a gift and simply keep them.

Chapter Six

"What happened to the dog?" Avery asked as they got into the car.

"He went home."

"To Jack?" Avery's voice was laced with disgust.

"Yes." Betty slowly pulled out of the garage.

"Did you talk to him first?"

"The dog?"

Avery laughed. "No, Grandma. I mean Jack. Did you talk to the beast? Did you tell him that he needs to take better care of his dog?"

"Not exactly." Betty sighed. "Would you mind hopping out and closing the garage door, dear?"

"Where's your remote?"

"What?"

"For the door."

"This is a very old-fashioned door."

Betty frowned as she waited for Avery to close the door. She felt like she was in over her head. Not just with Avery, but with Jack and the dog and just everything.

"Thank you," Betty said as Avery hopped back in the car.

"So, was Jack happy to see his dog?" Avery persisted.

"I...I don't know."

"What do you mean you don't know?"

"I mean I didn't actually see him."

"But you took the dog back?"

"Yes. He didn't answer the door." Betty considered explaining how she'd taken the dog back twice but figured that would only muddy the already murky waters.

"How could you possibly give the dog back without seeing his lame owner, Grandma?"

Betty grimaced. Why was this so complicated? "Avery..." Betty suddenly remembered a good distraction technique. "Did you remember to call your parents?"

"No..."

"Well, you promised me you'd do that."

"Can I use your phone?"

"Of course you can use my phone. I already told you that."

"Okay." Avery held out her hand.

"What?"

"Your phone."

"But it's not here, Avery. We're in the car." Betty wondered if the girl had lost her senses.

"You mean you don't have a cell phone?"

"Oh." Betty shook her head as she stopped for a red light. "No, of course not. Why would I need one of those foolish things?"

Avery looked astonished. "Are you serious?"

"Of course I'm serious. I do not understand what all the fuss is about. We've all gotten along fine without those little phones for a long time. In fact, I think people who use their phones in public—in restaurants or movie theaters or even church—well, they are very inconsiderate."

"You really are old-fashioned, Grandma."

Betty peered at Avery. "Shall I assume you have a cell phone?"

"The light's green."

Betty pulled forward.

"I *had* one. But I lost it."

"Oh yes, the great hitchhiking heist."

Avery laughed.

"Well, you must promise me that you'll call your parents as soon as we get home, Avery." They shook on it.

Avery shadowed Betty as they perused the party store for golden anniversary items. Betty had offered in early November to do this for Marsha and Jim. And she'd meant to take care of it long before now, but she'd been hit with a nasty cold that had hung on much longer than usual. She just hoped that she hadn't waited too late. Fortunately, she'd had the foresight to order the napkins earlier. She just hoped there would be no shortage on paper plates and cups now.

"How about helium balloons?" Avery asked.

"Balloons?" Betty looked up at the gaudily decorated Mylar confections displayed along the wall and frowned. There were rainbows, kitty cats, dinosaurs, and cartoon characters, but nothing very appropriate for a golden anniversary. "I don't think so, dear."

"Why not?" Avery reached into a basket of regular balloons. The old-fashioned kind. "You could do the plain metallic-gold ones mixed with some pearly whites. Put a bunch of them together in balloon bouquets. It would be pretty."

Betty considered this, trying not to look shocked as Avery raised the balloon to her lips and proceeded to inflate it.

"And cheap," Avery said as she proudly held up the filled balloon. It was actually rather attractive, and it did look like gold.

Betty nodded. "Yes, I suppose balloons might be nice after all."

"Where are you having this little shindig anyway?" Avery let go of the balloon and it went flying through the store, making a long series of sputtering sounds.

Betty looked over her shoulder nervously. "The church."

"Down in the basement?"

"Yes, of course. That's where we have social functions."

"Then you'll need lots of balloons and all kinds of things to brighten it up."

"I've only budgeted fifty dollars for this," Betty said.

"Fifty bucks?" Avery frowned. "For how many people?"

"We've estimated around eighty to a hundred. Fortunately, I've already paid for the napkins."

They headed to the paper plate section.

"So what all do you need to get with your fifty bucks?"

Betty pulled out her list. "Paper plates, coffee cups, plastic punch glasses, and forks. Oh yes, and a few decorations."

Avery picked up a package of gold paper plates and shook her head. "I'm not a math whiz, Grandma, but these plates alone are going to eat up a big chunk of your budget."

Betty felt a headache coming on. Avery was probably right. Oh, why hadn't she considered this earlier? "I suppose I'll just have to increase my budget."

"Or…"

"Or what?"

"Let me help you, Grandma."

Betty blinked. "That's very sweet, Avery. But how do you intend to help me?"

Avery got a sly look. "Back in high school, I loved doing set design in drama. I was always able to take a tiny budget and make it go a long way. Everyone was impressed. One year we did a pirate musical, and you should've seen how realistic it was."

Betty didn't know what drama or pirates had to do with golden anniversaries, but her head was beginning to throb more now. "I think I need an aspirin," she muttered as she opened her purse to peer inside.

"Are you sick?"

"Just a headache."

"I know," Avery said suddenly. "I saw a coffee shop next door. Why don't you go and sit down, take your aspirin, have a cup of coffee, and just relax. I'll do your shopping for you."

Betty knew this was a bad idea, but she didn't want to offend Avery. "Oh, I don't think that's necessary. I just—"

"No, Grandma." Avery snatched the list from Betty. "Let me do this for you. Just trust me, okay?"

Betty reached up and rubbed her temples.

"I promise you won't be disappointed."

"I just don't think it's a good idea, dear."

"You liked the balloon idea, didn't you?"

"Well, yes, but—"

"No buts."

Betty felt too flustered to think clearly. On one hand, it would be an enormous relief to hand this off to Avery, go and sit down, have a cup of tea, and take it easy. On the other hand, what if the whole thing turned into a complete mess?

"Really, Grandma, I *know* I can do this."

Avery's eyes were so bright and hopeful that Betty decided she wanted to give the girl this chance. Really, what could it hurt? So she opened her purse, extracted the money she had put into an envelope marked "Deerwoods' Fiftieth," and handed the bills to Avery.

"And I can go to Goodwill too," Avery said. "You know, to pick up some clothes."

"Oh, yes." Betty had nearly forgotten that part of the plan. She reached into her purse again and took out her old, worn billfold. She pulled out two twenty-dollar bills. She knew that wasn't much for clothes shopping, but it was the remainder of her December grocery money. Still, she thought that perhaps this month's budget would need to be increased a bit. After all, she hadn't planned on having a houseguest. She could make adjustments for it later. It was always such a challenge living on a fixed and very limited income. But she had made it this far in life, and always the good Lord provided.

"Here you go, dear. I hope you can stretch this."

"Now you just go next door and relax, Grandma. Let me take care of everything."

Betty closed her purse and nodded. But the

movement only made her head throb more. All she wanted was to sit down, take an aspirin, and sip a nice, hot cup of tea.

Before long, that was exactly what she was doing. And after about thirty minutes, she began to feel more like herself again.

"More hot water for your tea?" the middle-aged waitress asked.

Betty glanced at her watch. "Yes, I suppose that would be nice."

"Doing some Christmas shopping today?" The waitress refilled the metal teapot, snapping the lid shut.

"Not exactly." Betty smiled at her. She explained about her friends' fiftieth wedding anniversary and how her granddaughter had offered to help with the shopping.

"Your granddaughter must be delightful," the woman said. "What a relief when so many young people are so messed up. Did you hear the news today?"

"What's that?"

"Big drug bust over on 17th Street. Cocaine, meth, marijuana…there were even a bunch of firearms."

"In our town?" Betty clutched her coffee mug.

"Oh yeah." The waitress lowered her voice.

"I actually recognized one of the young men. He'd been in here a number of times. I never would've guessed he was involved in something like that." She shook her head. "You just never know."

"No, I suppose not." Of course, this only made Betty think about Jack Jones again. Suspicions such as these had gone through her head more than once in regard to him. For all she knew, he could've ripped the house apart in order to grow marijuana inside. She'd heard of things like that before. And what if he had guns? Oh, it was too horrible to think about.

But what about that poor dog? Perhaps she'd been cruel to leave him there with Jack. She hoped that Jack wasn't cruel to the poor animal. And then she thought about her granddaughter and how upset she would be if any harm came to that dog. What had Betty been thinking?

Betty looked at her watch again. She was surprised to see that an hour had passed with no sign of Avery. She finished the last sip of tea and wondered what she should do. The strip mall wasn't so large that Betty couldn't go look for Avery. But it was cold outside.

And what if Betty went to the wrong place and Avery showed up at the coffee shop?

"Everything okay?" the waitress asked with a concerned expression.

"Yes. I just thought my granddaughter would be finished by now."

"Have you tried to call her?"

Betty frowned. "No…but I'm sure she'll be along any minute now."

"Yes, I'm sure she will."

But as soon as the waitress returned to the kitchen, Betty began to get worried. Really, what did she know about Avery? She hadn't spent time with her in years. Betty knew that she'd run away from home. And she hadn't even called her parents to say she was alive. Then she'd hitchhiked with a friend, gotten her things stolen, and eventually wound up on Betty's doorstep. Not exactly the profile of a responsible young woman. And not exactly like the picture Betty had concocted for the waitress.

For all Betty knew, Avery could be involved in something horrible. Something frightening like drugs. And hadn't Betty just given Avery a handful of cash? What if Avery was long gone by now? What if she'd simply pocketed Betty's money and run?

Betty sighed. It wouldn't be the money so much. But to think that Avery had tricked her, deceived her into believing that she wanted to help, when she was really taking advantage of her...Well, it wasn't only disheartening; it made Betty feel sick. She closed her eyes and took a deep breath, willing herself to relax, to let these worries go, and to put her trust in God. It was an old habit she'd adopted long ago—a way of dealing with life's stresses.

As she sat there with her eyes closed, she heard the familiar strain of Bing Crosby crooning, "I'll be home for Christmas, you can count on me..." Funny how the old tunes from her era were becoming popular among young people again.

She relaxed as she listened to the words, remembering how she and Chuck had been separated for one Christmas while he was serving in Korea. How many times had she listened to the song and cried? But then he'd come home, they'd gotten married, and she had never again expected to be separated from him during the holidays. Little had she known that they would have only a dozen Christmases to share. And then he'd be gone.

The song ended, and Betty opened her eyes to discover that her cheeks were damp with tears. Embarrassed by this display of emotion, she quickly reached for the paper napkin and dabbed at her face. So silly, after all these years, to still be missing him like that.

She sighed and looked outside. It was starting to get dusky, and she had told Avery she wanted to be home while it was still light since she didn't see well after dark. She put out the money to pay for her tea and slowly stood.

"No sign of your granddaughter yet?" The waitress frowned.

Betty just shook her head and slowly walked toward the door. It felt as if someone had tied large rocks around her ankles. And she knew she was a very foolish old woman to have trusted Avery like that. At least she hadn't given her the car keys. That was something to be thankful for.

Chapter Seven

"Grandma!" Avery called. She rushed toward the coffee shop with what looked like dozens of shopping bags hanging from her shoulders, arms, and hands.

"Avery!" Betty couldn't believe her eyes. "Where have you been?"

"Shopping, of course."

"But you took so long." Betty peered at her. "How did you manage to buy so much… stuff?"

"Goodwill, the Dollar Store, and a craft shop around the corner."

"Oh?" Betty opened the trunk of her car, watching as Avery piled in her purchases.

"Yeah. I found all sorts of cool things, Grandma. It's going to be so awesome."

Betty blinked to see some magenta and

lime-colored artificial flowers tumbling out of a large plastic bag. She couldn't imagine what those bright blooms might be for—perhaps a Mexican fiesta. But they certainly weren't appropriate for a dignified fiftieth anniversary party. Even so, she was so relieved to see Avery again, to know that she hadn't run off and that she actually had been shopping—well, Betty didn't even care what kind of frivolities Avery had wasted her money on. At least she was safe.

Avery was very secretive about her purchases when they got home. She asked if she could keep the decorations in her room while she worked on them. Betty had no idea what that meant, but she was too tired to protest, so she agreed.

"But don't forget your promise," Betty said. "To call your parents."

"Yeah." Avery nodded as she went into her room. "I'll do it."

"I'm going to begin fixing dinner. I have decided that I'll do the cooking and you'll be on cleanup. Does that sound fair?"

Avery grinned. "Sure. I love your cooking, Grandma."

Betty smiled. Maybe Avery hadn't changed that much after all. Still, it was a bit stressful having a young person suddenly thrust into your life. One didn't know what to expect, how to react.

Tonight Betty was making macaroni and cheese, but not the boxed kind that turned out orange and salty. Avery had talked her into getting some of the boxed kind at the store when she'd been visiting Betty one summer. One bite and Betty had decided that Avery needed to learn a better way. Avery had been cautious at first, complaining that Betty's macaroni "looked funny," but after she tasted it, she declared it to be the "bestest macaroni and cheese ever." Betty made it with real cheese and butter and cream, and she always baked it in the oven, removing the foil for the last few minutes so the bread crumbs turned crispy and golden brown. Betty hadn't made macaroni and cheese in ages, but her mouth was watering when she finally slid the heavy casserole dish into the oven.

She looked at her messy kitchen, then smiled to herself. This was one of the benefits of having Avery here. Betty could cook what she liked, and her granddaughter would clean up the mess. Not a bad little setup.

"Grandma," Avery said from the living

room. "Someone's at the door. Want me to get it?"

"I'm coming." Betty untied her apron and went out to see who was there. It was nearly six now, and most respectable people would be having dinner.

"Oh!" Avery said. She opened the front door wide enough for Betty to see Jack standing there, a somber expression on his face and a familiar-looking garbage bag in his hand. The dog stood at his feet, wagging his tail and looking into the house like he expected to be invited in for dinner.

"What do you want?" Avery put her hands on her hips and scowled at Jack.

Jack studied her for a moment, then turned toward Betty. "I don't know what your game is, but I do not want a dog."

Avery stepped forward and stared up into Jack's face. "Seems like you should've thought of that sooner."

"Huh?" He frowned. "Who are you anyway?"

"This is my granddaughter, Avery," Betty said. "Avery, I'd like you to meet my neighbor Jack."

"I know all about you, Jack," Avery said.

"I wanted to report you to the Humane Society, but Grandma wouldn't let me."

"What?"

Avery pointed down at the dog. "You're a grown man. You should know better than to treat an animal the way you've treated him. He's a sweet dog, and you have totally neglected and—"

"You're crazy," he said. "This isn't my dog."

"He was filthy and cold and half-starved and—"

"And he's not my dog," Jack said. He looked over at Betty again. "I thought he was your dog. I saw him in your yard."

"And I saw him in your yard," Betty said. "I assumed he belonged to you."

"Looks like we both assumed wrong." Jack dropped the plastic bag in her house. "Here you go."

"What do you mean, 'here you go'?" Betty said.

"You got him this stuff." Jack glared at her. "I guess that means he belongs to you."

"He does *not* belong to me." Betty stepped closer, glaring back at him now.

"Looks to me like he does. You got him the collar and leash and—"

"But he is *not* my dog. I only got those things because I thought you were—"

"So you admit that you purchased the dog paraphernalia?"

"I felt sorry for the dog."

"And they say possession is nine-tenths of the law, right?"

Betty didn't know how to respond.

He kicked the plastic bag with the toe of his boot. "So this is your dog bed, and that must mean this is your dog."

"But I don't want a—"

"I'd appreciate it if you'd quit dropping your dog off at my house." He narrowed his eyes at Betty. "And if you do it again, I will report *you* to the Humane Society. Do you understand?"

Betty was too angry to respond.

"We understand," Avery snapped, "that you are a selfish, mean man. And you don't deserve a dog like this." She reached down and picked up the mutt, holding him protectively in her arms. "He is lucky to escape you."

"You got that right!" Jack turned and slammed the door shut behind him.

"What a beast!" Avery said.

"Good riddance," Betty said.

"You poor thing," Avery cooed to the dog. "I'll bet you're hungry."

Betty just stared at her granddaughter and the dog. She wanted to tell Avery in no uncertain terms that the dog was not welcome in her home. But Avery looked so happy and hopeful that Betty just couldn't bring herself to say those words. Not yet anyway. Besides, there wasn't much they could do about the situation tonight. The animal shelter would probably be closed by now. And Betty didn't like to drive after dark anyway. She would deal with the dog tomorrow.

"Don't forget to call your parents," Betty said as she headed back to the kitchen to make a salad.

While Betty was in the kitchen, she overheard Avery talking on the phone. She could tell she was talking to her mother and that it wasn't an easy conversation.

"I want to stay *here* for Christmas," Avery said. There was a long pause, and Betty imagined what Stephanie was probably saying to her daughter. So often she had used accusatory words, negativity, blame, and guilt to pressure her daughter into complying with her wishes. Betty had witnessed these awkward conversations before. But because Stephanie wasn't her daughter and Betty had no actual blood relation to Avery, she had always kept her mouth shut. Still, it had troubled her. It seemed unhealthy. And sad.

"I'm a grown-up," Avery said. "And I can—" She was obviously cut off again. No surprises there. "I'm sorry you feel that way, Mother. Merry Christmas to you!" There was a loud bang as Avery slammed the receiver down. Good thing that old phone was tough.

"My mother is a moron," Avery said as she joined Betty in the kitchen. "Man, something smells really good in here." She peeked in the oven. "Mac and cheese?"

"Yes. I was hankering for some."

Avery smacked her lips. "All right."

"So…how are your parents?" Betty asked with hesitation.

"I don't know about Gary. But my mom is as messed up as ever."

"I'm sure they've been worried about you."

"My mom is more worried about how it looks to have a missing daughter." Avery began to imitate her mother. "'Oh dear, what *will* people think if Avery is still AWOL at Christmas? It will completely ruin our hallowed Christmas celebrations if Avery doesn't show up looking like the perfect little princess daughter. Oh my, we must keep up appearances.'"

Betty smiled. Avery actually did sound a lot like Stephanie. Not that Betty intended to say as much.

"I gave the dog some food, Grandma. But he hasn't even touched it. Do you think he's okay?"

"I have no idea. I've never had a dog before."

"Me neither. But he's so sweet. If he really doesn't belong to Jack, I think I'll keep him."

As they set the table together, Betty wanted to point out how unrealistic Avery's adopt-a-dog plan was, but she decided to hold her tongue for now. Of course, the dog would need to go to the animal shelter tomorrow. But Betty would see to that. In the meantime, it wouldn't hurt to postpone that conversation. And Avery seemed so happy tonight, chatting cheerfully as they ate dinner. Betty felt there was no sense in hurrying up what would surely come as a disappointment later.

While Avery was cleaning up the dinner things, the phone rang. Betty always had a tendency to jump when the phone rang. Maybe it was because she didn't get that many calls in the evening. Or maybe it was just an old reaction from a time when a ringing phone could bring bad news. But she hurried to pick up the extension in the hallway, out of the noise of the kitchen.

"Hi, Mom."

"Oh, Gary." Betty smiled as she sat in the straight-backed chair. "It's so nice to hear your voice."

"You too. I hear that Avery paid you a surprise visit."

"Yes, she's here. And I'm thoroughly enjoying her."

"I'm sure she's enjoying you too." There was a pause, and Betty thought she could hear another voice in the background. "But, uh, Stephanie is not too happy."

"Oh?"

"She really wants Avery home for Christmas."

"That's what Avery said."

"And she wants me to tell you that you should send her home."

"I should *send* her home?" Betty blinked as she imagined packing her granddaughter in a large cardboard box and shipping her out to Atlanta on a UPS truck.

"Naturally, we'll pay for her airline ticket,"

he said quickly. "But if you could just make Avery see that she needs to—"

"I doubt that I can *make* Avery do anything she doesn't want to do."

"Okay, Mom, *make* was not the right word. But I know that you could influence her. Avery would listen to you."

"Avery is an adult, Gary."

"An adult who can act very childish."

"Perhaps she acts childish because she is so often treated as a child."

There was a long pause. "You make a good point."

"Avery seems to want to stay here," Betty said. "She has offered to help me with the Deerwoods' fiftieth anniversary celebration."

"They've been married fifty years?"

"Yes." Betty wanted to point out that she and Gary's father would've been beyond that milestone by now if Chuck was still alive. But she realized there was no reason to.

"Tell them congratulations for me."

"I will. But, you see, Avery has helped me to get things. And she's going to work on them and—"

"Sorry, Mom," he said quickly. "But Stephanie wants the phone. Do you mind talking to her?"

"Not at all." But Betty wasn't the one to do the talking. When Stephanie got on the other end, she immediately began to rant and rave about how Avery needed to come home—right now. About how she'd been gone away too long. And about how it was wrong for Betty to keep her away from her family.

"Excuse me," Betty said. "I am *not* keeping Avery from anyone."

"You're making it easier for her to avoid facing up to her responsibilities."

"Her responsibilities?"

"To her family."

"What responsibilities does she have to her family?"

"To be here with us. To be with our friends. It's what we do every year. Avery knows that."

"But Avery is an adult," she said for the second time. "She should be able to make up her own mind about—"

"Avery has the mind of a child," Stephanie snapped. "She proved that by running off and doing God only knows what with God only knows who."

"That may be. But she's here with me now. She's in no danger."

"And I suppose you can promise me that,

Betty? You're prepared to take personal responsibility for my daughter's welfare?"

"I'm only saying that she is just fine. And she's welcome to stay with me for as long as—"

"So you're choosing her side. You're taking a stand against me while you enable her."

Betty wasn't exactly sure what *enabling* meant these days, but the way Stephanie slung the term, like it was an accusation, worried Betty. Why didn't game shows like *Jeopardy* talk about words like this? Just the same, Betty decided to give it a try. "Wouldn't *enabling* mean that I'm *helping* a person to do something…as in making them *able*?"

Stephanie laughed so loudly that Betty's ear rang, and she had to hold the receiver away. "Of course that's what you'd think, Betty. But no, enabling is making it easy for a person to avoid what they really need to be doing. You enable them to fail."

"Oh." Betty had no response to that.

"But if you're determined to position yourself between us and Avery"—Stephanie made a sniffling sound, although Betty did not think she was really crying—"then I suppose I can't stop you."

"I'm not taking a position," Betty said.

"Oh yes you are."

"I've simply told Avery she can stay with me through the holidays if she wants to and—"

"Fine. Have it your way. I hope you both have a very merry Christmas!" Of course, with the tone of her voice and the way she said this, she could've been using foul language and the meaning would not have been much different. And before Betty could respond, she heard the dull buzz of the dial tone in her ear.

"Let me guess," Avery said as she appeared in the hallway with a dish towel hanging limply in her hand. "My mom?"

Betty just nodded as she replaced the phone.

"Now she's mad at you too?"

"I'm afraid so."

Avery grinned. "Well, join the club, Grandma."

"Apparently my dues are all paid up in full."

"My mother would've made a good dictator."

Betty stifled a smile.

"She wants to rule the world, you know."

"I just hope you're sure you're making the right decision to stay here for the holidays."

Avery frowned. "You don't want me?"

Betty hesitated. Of course she wanted her. But was she wrong to keep Avery from returning home? Was she an enabler—the bad kind?

"I'll leave if you want me to," Avery said quietly.

"No, of course I don't want you to leave." Betty put a hand on her shoulder. "I only want what's best for you, dear."

Avery nodded, but there was a flicker of hurt in her eyes. Betty wondered if she should say more to reassure her granddaughter. But what could she say? It was true that Betty only wanted what was best for Avery. The problem was that Betty didn't have a clue as to what that was. Should Avery stay here and risk angering her mother? Or go home and face whatever it was she needed to face? Really, what was best? And it seemed unlikely that an old woman like herself—living on a very frugal budget and on the verge of selling her home and fleeing from a questionable neighborhood—was truly the best resource for someone like Avery.

Chapter Eight

The next morning, Betty got up at her usual time, just a bit past seven. But when she went to the laundry room to check on the dog, she was surprised to discover that he was not there. The door was firmly shut, just like it had been last night, and his bed and food dishes were still there, but the dog was missing. Betty checked around the house and even looked out into the backyard, but the mutt was nowhere to be seen.

Finally, worried that Jack had sneaked over and broken into her house in the middle of the night, she decided to check on the welfare of her granddaughter. And there, in the guest bed, were both Avery and the dog. The dog looked up from where he was comfortably curled up against Avery's back, but Avery continued to snooze. Betty just shook her head and quietly closed the door. She hoped the dog didn't have fleas.

Thanks to the dog's need to go outside, Avery got up before eight. Betty sipped her coffee, watching as Avery waited by the sliding door for the dog to finish up his business. To Betty's relief he had found another part of the yard—not the dogwood tree—to relieve himself this time.

"It's freezing out there," Avery said as she let the dog back inside. "Do you think it'll snow?"

"I'm sure it's a possibility." Betty set her coffee mug down.

"I've always wanted to see a white Christmas," she said dreamily. "Maybe this will be the year."

"Maybe." Betty smiled at Avery. "Now, if you don't mind, I'd like to hear more about what you got for the Deerwoods' anniversary party."

Avery's mouth twisted to one side. "But I wanted to surprise you, Grandma."

"Surprise me?"

"Yes. I have to work on everything. But I don't want you to see it until I'm done."

"That's very sweet of you, dear. But I'd

really like to have some sort of an idea of what you're—"

"I used your list," Avery said. "And I can guarantee you that I got enough plates and cups and things for a hundred people. And I've got what I need for decorations too. So can't you just let me work on it and surprise you? I promise you it'll be awesome. You won't be disappointed."

Betty thought of those loud magenta and lime flowers she'd spied in the trunk and wasn't so sure. What if the Deerwood party turned into a luau or a fiesta or a pirate party? How would Betty explain it?

"Please?" Avery asked.

Betty remembered how many times Avery's mother had questioned Avery's abilities, belittled her skills, and treated her like a child. "All right." Betty nodded. "I will trust you with this, Avery."

Avery threw her arms around Betty. "Thank you, Grandma! I won't let you down."

After breakfast, Avery remained barricaded in her room. Occasionally, she'd emerge in search of things like glue, scissors, staplers, and tape. Sometimes she would carry plastic bags out to the garage, warning Betty not to come out and peek while she worked on something out there. Avery reminded Betty of some mad scientist, secretly creating…what? Frankenstein? A bomb? Hopefully the Deerwoods' fiftieth anniversary would survive whatever it was she was putting together.

To distract herself, Betty decided to proceed with her Christmas baking. Just as she was attempting to fit a pan of fudge into the fridge, she felt a nudge on the back of her leg. She jumped and nearly dropped the pan before she realized it was the dog.

"Oh!" she exclaimed. "You scared me."

The dog looked hopefully at her, wagging his tail, then he ran toward the sliding glass door.

"You need to go out?" she said as she slid the fudge pan onto the lower shelf. "I'm coming, I'm coming." She opened the door and let the dog out, but as she was waiting she heard the oven timer ring. She hurried back to the kitchen, worried that her walnut squares might be getting overdone, which would ruin them completely. But she removed the pan to see that they looked just about perfect. And smelled even better.

She got out the waxed paper, tore off a sheet, and laid it on the cutting board. Then she sifted a layer of powdered sugar onto this and went back to see that the pan had cooled just slightly, so she carefully turned it upside down and dumped the squares onto the waxed paper. She sifted more powdered sugar over the top while the squares were still warm.

Finally they were finished. She couldn't resist trying a square just to be sure. And then, of course, she needed a cup of coffee to go with it. She poured the last one from the morning pot, then sat down to enjoy this lovely little treat.

She had just finished it up when she looked out into the backyard to realize that the dog didn't appear to be there. She stood and looked more closely, peering to the left and the right. Then she went outside to call for him. But he didn't come. That's when she noticed the hole in the back fence. Had the foolish dog gone off and wandered into Jack's yard again? She peered into Jack's yard, which was just as messy as ever, but she didn't see any sign of the dog. Still, she felt certain that was where he had gone.

Betty returned to the house and wondered what to do. Really, the sooner she took the dog to the pound, the better they'd all be. Besides, it had occurred to her that it was entirely possible the dog already had an owner who was looking for him. In the meantime, she didn't want to give Jack enough time to follow through with last night's threat to call the Humane Society and turn her in as a negligent pet owner. Not that he could prove such an outrageous accusation, but even so, she didn't wish to invite trouble.

She got her walking jacket and the dog leash, and on her way through the kitchen she paused to look at the walnut squares. Suddenly she remembered what her daughter Susan had said: "Kill him with kindness." Fine, that was just what she would do. Or at least try.

Betty got into her holiday cupboard, dug out a festive plastic Christmas plate, and carefully arranged walnut squares and fudge on it. It would've been prettier with a few more kinds of cookies, but this would have to do. She covered it tightly with plastic wrap and hoped that this would do the trick. Then she slipped on her gloves, and armed with leash and cookies, she was ready for her mission.

Before she left, she knocked on Avery's door.

"Don't come in!" Avery yelled.

"I won't. I'm just going next door."

"Okay!"

Betty considered giving her granddaughter a fuller explanation about the missing dog but didn't want to involve her in what could easily turn into another nasty dispute. Who knew how Jack would react? Would he assume that Betty had purposely sent the dog to his house in order to harass him? Just what she didn't need right now. Hopefully her sugary peace offering would help to smooth things over.

As she walked to Jack's house, Betty wondered how she might use the dog's runabout habits to her advantage today. She was well aware that Avery wanted to keep the dog. But perhaps she could convince her that the reason the dog had run away was to search for its real owner. And that the responsible thing to do was to reunite the mutt with his family. Surely Avery would understand.

Today Jack's front yard was cluttered with what appeared to be the Spencers' old wall-to-wall carpeting. Betty frowned down at a strip of olive-green rug. Gladys had always kept her home immaculate, and Betty suspected that the carpet still had many years of serviceable use left in it. Not that Jack seemed to care about such things.

Not for the first time, Betty was curious as to the interior state of the house. She stepped over the carpet strip and rang the doorbell. She could hear a power tool running inside, whirring noisily. She rang the bell again and then knocked. But the sound of the machine continued steadily, and Betty knew that it was hopeless. She was tempted to try the door but knew that could easily backfire. The last thing she needed was for Jack to accuse her of breaking and entering.

She considered leaving the cookie plate behind, but Jack would probably assume it was one of his neighbors attempting to poison him and toss it into the trash. And she wasn't about to waste perfectly good cookies.

Why was this so frustrating?

She turned on her heel and marched back to her house. Really, why did she even bother? As for the dog, well, he was on his own as far as Betty was concerned.

"Where's Ralph?" Avery asked as Betty came into the house.

"Ralph?" Betty set the cookie plate aside and removed her gloves.

"The dog."

"You named him Ralph?" Betty blinked. "Why?"

"It was my grandpa's name."

"Oh. Well…" Betty hung up her coat.

"I looked in the laundry room and in the backyard, but I didn't see him anywhere. Do you know where he is?" Avery looked worried.

"I was looking for him myself. I thought maybe he'd gone to Jack's house."

"Did he?"

"I don't know for sure. Jack's not answering his door."

"But you think Ralph is there?"

Betty shrugged. "Or perhaps he ran away to search for his owner."

"His owner?" Avery scowled. "Do you really think Ralph has an owner, Grandma? He looked like he'd been abandoned or was a runaway."

"Or maybe he's just lost. It occurred to me that he could have a family who loves him. Someone might be looking for him."

"He didn't have a collar. And you said there'd been a string tied around his neck, almost like someone wanted to strangle him."

"We don't know that for sure, Avery."

"Well, I'm going out to look for him." Avery reached for the door.

"Wear a coat," Betty told her. "It's freezing out there."

So Avery grabbed her coat, took the leash,

and then was gone. Betty stood by Avery's closed bedroom door and considered taking a peek, but she knew that would offend her granddaughter. Instead, she returned to her baking.

She was just rolling out sugar cookie dough when Avery appeared—with the dog. "I found Ralph!" she said.

Betty peered down at the dog. He was wagging his tail happily, sniffing the floor and eagerly licking up spilled crumbs from Betty's baking spree. "Where did you find him?"

"You were right, Grandma." Avery tossed her parka over a kitchen chair. "He was at Jack's house."

"Jack answered the door?"

"Nope."

Betty frowned.

"I rang the bell and knocked, and finally I just opened the door and went in."

"You went *into* Jack's house?" Betty's hand flew to her mouth.

"Yep. Walked right in. Man, what a mess."

"What was going on inside?"

"Major demolition."

"He's tearing the place apart?"

"It sure looked like it."

"Did you see anything, uh, unusual?" Betty

wanted to ask specifically about dangerous things like drugs or firearms, but knew that sounded a bit paranoid.

"I didn't get far enough to see much."

"Jack stopped you?"

"Yeah. But not before I spotted Ralph."

Betty shook her head.

"So I snatched up Ralph and gave Jack a piece of my mind."

"Oh dear."

"I told Jack that he was rude and selfish and mean, and that you were a nice person and that he had no right to make your life miserable."

Betty held on to a kitchen chair to brace herself. "You said all that?"

"I sure did."

"Oh my."

Avery took a piece of cookie dough and popped it in her mouth. "Yum!"

"And what did Jack say to you?" Betty asked. "I mean in response to all you said to him?"

Avery laughed. "Nothing. I think he was speechless."

"Did you ask him why he let the dog in his house?"

"I accused him of dognapping."

"Dognapping?"

"Yeah. I told him since he'd made it clear that Ralph didn't belong to him, he had no right taking him into his house."

"I am curious as to why he'd do that. Especially after all he said last night. He seemed to genuinely dislike the dog."

Avery nodded. "Yeah. I think it's suspicious, Grandma. I don't trust Jack."

Now Betty remembered her previous strategy. "But I'm also curious as to why the dog took off like that, Avery. It makes me think that he could be looking for his family."

"We're his family now, Grandma."

Betty frowned. "But what if someone out there is missing him, Avery? Perhaps a family with children? What if they want their pup home for Christmas?"

Avery bit her lip.

"We wouldn't want to be responsible for someone's sorrow."

Avery nodded. "You're right. I'll make 'found dog' posters. I'll put them in the neighborhood and—"

"But I thought we should take him to the dog shelter."

Avery shook her head stubbornly. "No, that would be cruel."

Betty didn't know what to say.

"Let me handle this, Grandma. Please."

Betty looked down at the dog and sighed. "I'll tell you what, Avery. I'll give you until the weekend to find his owners."

Avery nodded. "Okay. I'll do my best."

"In the meantime, the dog—"

"Ralph."

"Fine. In the meantime, Ralph will be your responsibility."

"No problem."

"And I suggest you fix that hole in the fence unless you want to go looking for him at Jack's house again."

"I'll handle it." Avery reached for another clump of cookie dough and popped it in her mouth, then turned to the dog. "Come on, Ralph."

Betty watched as the dog, tail wagging, followed Avery out of the kitchen just like he'd been doing it his whole life. Still, this was not reassuring. Already it seemed that Avery had bonded with the dog. What would happen when she'd be forced to part with him?

Chapter Nine

Avery, true to her word, made "found dog" posters and hung them around the neighborhood. But, just to be sure, Betty called the animal shelter and local vets to let them know about Ralph as well. Naturally, she did this while Avery was holed up in her room, where she was working on the anniversary things and unable to hear. But so far there hadn't been a single inquiry about the dog. Betty didn't know what to make of it.

Then late on Thursday afternoon, the dog went missing again. Avery was fit to be tied, and Betty felt a mixture of relief and regret. On one hand, it would be easier for everyone if the dog simply exited their lives as quickly as he'd entered. Yet at the same time, Betty realized she'd grown a tad bit fond of the mutt. She didn't mind when he nestled down at her feet while she sat at the kitchen table. And she liked how nicely he would sit to wait for a treat—just like someone had taught him manners. Sometimes she thought he was a right nice little dog. This, of course, worried her—she had no intention of becoming attached to a pet.

"I'll bet Jack took him again," Avery said as she pulled on her parka. "I'm going to find out."

"I don't think you should go alone." Betty pushed herself up from her recliner.

"You sit tight, Grandma," Avery said. "I can handle this."

Betty wasn't so sure. "But Jack is a bit unpredictable, dear."

"I can deal with him."

"Wait," Betty said. "Why don't you take him a cookie plate?"

"A cookie plate?" Avery frowned. "Why would I want to do that?"

Betty took Avery by the elbow and walked her to the kitchen as she explained the "kill him with kindness" theory. "Your aunt Susan reminded me of it a few days ago. And I think it's worth a try."

"I don't know."

But Betty was already loading up a Christmas platter. "I don't think it could hurt," she said as she wrapped it in plastic wrap. "And if it doesn't sweeten him up, well, at least we can tell Susan that we gave it a try."

"Okay." But as Avery took the plate, she still looked skeptical.

"Are you sure you don't want me to come along?"

"No, I'll be fine."

"Just be careful." Betty shook her finger in warning.

"Yeah, yeah." Avery was already halfway out the door.

Betty sighed as she returned to her recliner and the task of untangling an old string of Christmas lights. Earlier that morning Avery had decided to venture into the attic, then happily came down with two boxes of Christmas decorations. After that, she'd been determined that the house should be decorated to the hilt.

At first, Betty had opposed the idea. She had imagined being alone when it was time to take everything down, struggling to get it all put away before her trip to Florida. However, it wasn't long before the youthful enthusiasm infected Betty, and it was fun to see Avery enjoying herself. Betty watched with fascination as her granddaughter tried out new ways of using old decorations. For instance, Betty never would've hung her mother's old handblown glass ornaments on the dining room chandelier, but they actually looked quite lovely there, reflecting and refracting the light. Very clever indeed.

Betty set aside the hopelessly tangled lights and frowned out the front window. Had she been foolish to allow her granddaughter to go to that man's house? She got up and hurried to the kitchen, nervously staring at Jack's mess of a house as if she thought she could help Avery should trouble erupt. Just then the phone rang, and she was forced to turn away from the window.

She'd barely said hello when the female voice on the other end demanded to know if Avery was there.

"Hello, Stephanie," Betty said cheerfully, hoping she could warm up her daughter-in-law. "How are you doing, dear?"

"How do you think I'm doing when my only daughter refuses to come home for Christmas?"

"I really don't see why that should be such an—"

"That's just it. You really don't see, do you, Betty?"

"Avery is a grown woman, Stephanie. Shouldn't she be allowed to make her own choices about where—"

"Talk to your son," Stephanie snapped.

And then Gary was on the line. "Hi, Mom," he said.

"Hello, Gary."

"Stephanie wants me to persuade you to send Avery home."

"Is that what you want too?"

"I suppose." His voice sounded flat.

"But why? I don't understand why it's so important."

He didn't answer right away, and when he did, his voice was quiet. "Stephanie's mom is coming for Christmas. And, as you know, Evelyn is, uh, well, rather jealous."

"Oh?" Betty was well aware that Evelyn had often resented Betty's relationship with Avery in the past. But that was when Avery had been a little girl, a long time ago.

"I know it probably sounds silly to you."

"I just don't really understand."

"Well, Evelyn wants us to help her with her will. And Stephanie is worried that if Avery isn't here, and if Evelyn figures out that she's with you…well, Stephanie feels this could present a problem."

Betty was speechless. Did they plan to use Avery as some sort of bargaining chip, a form of insurance to assure them they would be properly compensated for in Evelyn's will? This just seemed so ridiculous.

"I know what you're thinking, Mom."

"Really?"

"I can guess."

"Well, I must admit that I'm a bit surprised."

"Anyway, I'm not telling you what to do." His voice was gentle now. More like the old Gary. "I'm just telling you how it is here. Frankly, I'm glad that Avery is with you. I think you're a wholesome influence in her life."

"Well, thank you."

"I just wanted you to know that Steph is very determined."

"I see."

"So if Avery could give her a call, just talk things through, I'd appreciate it."

"I'll tell Avery."

"And I apologize for how Steph just spoke to you. All I can say is that she's very upset. And she's been hurt deeply by Avery's little disappearing act."

"I'm sure it's been difficult for her."

"But I realize Avery is an adult. At least according to her birth date."

"If it's any encouragement, Avery is acting very much like an adult." Betty described how Avery had taken full responsibility for the anniversary preparations and how she'd put up "found dog" posters. "And this morning she even got me to help in decorating the house for Christmas. I'd been feeling a bit like Scrooge. But she's so enthusiastic that I finally gave in. And she's actually quite clever." Betty rambled on until Gary said he needed to go.

"I'll tell Avery to call her mother," Betty said. Then she hung up and looked out across the backyard toward Jack's house. It was dusky now, and suddenly Betty felt concerned. How long had Avery been gone? Shouldn't she be back by now? Betty could see light coming from what had once been the dining room window. But there was something like a sheet draped over it, so she couldn't see inside.

Betty began pacing in the kitchen. Should she go and check on the girl? Or would that seem like interfering? Would it send the message that Avery wasn't mature? That she wasn't capable of taking care of herself?

Betty looked up at the clock. It was about four forty now. Perhaps she should wait until five. But what might happen in twenty minutes? And then, if something really was wrong, wouldn't it be foolish for Betty to go over there? Wouldn't it be better to call the police? But if she called the police, what would she say to them? That her grown granddaughter had been at the neighbor's house for more than thirty minutes? They'd probably just laugh or write her off as crazy.

She considered calling the Gilmores, but what would she say to them? Katie was already fearful about Jack. Why alarm them further? Or maybe Katie and the girls had fled to her mother's by now. In that case, what would Betty say to poor Martin? He'd already endured several confrontations with their contrary neighbor. Why would he want to have another?

Betty continued to pace, staring out the window and trying to replace her worry with prayer. But her prayers sounded feeble. "Protect Avery," she said again and again.

Finally, it was nearly five o'clock, and she could stand it no longer. She went for her coat and took off to discover what was wrong. If all else failed, she might be able to scream loudly enough to disturb a neighbor. But Betty had barely rounded the corner when she spied Avery and the dog strolling her way.

"What happened?" Betty said. "Are you okay?"

"Sure." Avery smiled.

"But you were gone so long." Betty realized that her hands were shaking. Perhaps it was from the cold, but she thought otherwise.

"You were right, Grandma."

"Right?"

"Jack seemed to appreciate the cookies."

"Really?" Betty wasn't sure how to respond. She should be happy about that, but instead she felt suspicious.

"And we had a nice talk."

"Is that so?" Betty imagined Jack's dark countenance as he eyed her granddaughter. Sizing her up, making his plans for evil. Avery was a beautiful young woman. And vulnerable too. What if Jack were a rapist, a serial killer, or both? Oh, why had Betty been such a fool as to let her go over there by herself?

"He's lonely, Grandma."

"Is that what he told you?"

"Yes, and—"

"I don't want you going over there by yourself again," Betty said quickly. "I'm afraid he could be dangerous and—"

"He's not dangerous." Avery laughed.

"You don't know that."

"Oh, Grandma, you're just being paranoid. Jack told me about the misunderstandings you've had and how he's tried to talk sense into you, but how you just won't listen, and now the whole neighborhood has turned against him."

"And you believe him?" Betty stopped walking and turned to peer at Avery. Her face was illuminated by the streetlight, and she looked confused.

"Why shouldn't I believe him?"

"Because he's not trustworthy, Avery."

"But you're the one who said to be kind to him. And I think that's just what he needed."

Betty was too flustered to respond. So they both walked back to the house with only the clicking of the dog's toenails on the sidewalk to break the silence.

Why hadn't Betty seen the danger in this situation? Why had she allowed Avery to walk right into what could have easily been a trap? Wasn't that how criminals worked?

They earned the victim's trust, and then they went to work. What would Avery's mother think if she knew?

"Your mother called," Betty said as they went into the house.

"So?"

"She wants you to call her back." Betty removed her jacket. "She said it's urgent."

"Big surprise there."

"But you'll call her, won't you?"

"I guess."

"I promised that you would."

Avery groaned. "I wish she'd just leave me alone."

"I'm going to start dinner," Betty said. She headed for the kitchen, but once she got there, she just stood and looked out the window toward Jack's house. As she looked, it appeared more frightening and sinister than ever. And so she prayed again. Only this time she prayed that somehow Stephanie would convince her daughter to come home for Christmas. And, as much as Betty would miss the girl, she felt certain that Avery would be safer there than here.

Because they'd had a good-sized lunch, with a snack of Christmas cookies and tea in midafternoon, Betty decided to fix oatmeal for dinner. This with whole wheat toast and home-canned peaches should be sufficient for both of them. She was just taking the oatmeal off the stove when Avery appeared.

"My mother is losing her mind." Avery sat down at the kitchen table, which Betty had already set for their simple meal.

"How so?" Betty avoided Avery's eyes as she spooned the hot cereal into the bowls.

"She says Grandma Evelyn is dying."

"Is she?"

"I seriously don't think so."

Betty sat down, bowed her head, and asked the blessing. Then she looked at Avery. "So why does your mother think Evelyn is dying?"

"Because she's old."

Betty nodded. "But what if your mother is right?"

Avery just shrugged and stuck her spoon into the brown sugar, dumping two heaping spoonfuls onto her oatmeal.

"Would you feel bad if you didn't get to see your grandmother...if she were to die?"

"I guess."

Betty felt a stab of guilt. She knew she was being somewhat insincere with her granddaughter. But she was doing it for Avery's own good. She wanted Avery out of harm's way. More specifically, out of Jack's way.

"I still regret not making one last trip out to see my own mother," Betty said slowly. "I knew she'd been having some health problems, but I just didn't believe it was terribly serious. I considered going out to visit in June. But then I changed my mind. I don't even recall why exactly. The next thing I knew, she was gone. I never got another chance."

Avery nodded. "I'm sorry."

"Thank you, dear."

"But that was your mother. Not your grandmother."

"That's true."

"And I assume you had a good relationship with her?"

"Yes, very good."

"Well, it's not like that with me and my grandmother."

"Perhaps that's an even better reason to spend time with her."

"So that she can torture me?"

Betty didn't know what to say.

"Grandma Evelyn and my mom will probably gang up on me, Grandma. They'll get on my case for taking off. They'll lecture me about going back to school. They'll remind me that I'm a failure, and then they'll rub my nose in it." Avery seemed on the verge of tears now. She set down her spoon with a clank. "And I just can't take that—that's not a happy way to spend Christmas." She scooted her chair back and ran out of the kitchen, slamming her bedroom door behind her.

Betty felt like a villain. And her few bites of oatmeal now sat like hard little stones in her stomach. She just sat there with her hands laid flat on the kitchen table and wondered how she had managed to make such a mess of things. How was it possible to hurt someone so deeply when you only wished to help them?

Betty realized she was crying for the second time in one week. The tears surprised her. She was a woman who usually kept her emotions in check. But what surprised her even more was the feeling of something warm pressing against her leg. She looked down to see the dog sitting right next to her, looking up at her with the most compassionate brown eyes she'd ever seen.

Reaching down, she stroked his smooth head. "You really are a good dog, aren't you?" She stood slowly. "But there is someone else who needs you more than I do right now. Come on, boy." He obediently followed as she walked to Avery's room and quietly opened the door. Betty let him into the darkened room, where the quiet sobs of a hurting girl cut through her like a knife. She knew the animal's presence would just be a Band-Aid—a temporary solution to a problem that was much bigger than a little brown dog. But at the moment, it was all Betty had to offer.

Chapter Ten

Avery's mother called again the next morning. Betty tried not to eavesdrop as she took over the chore of cleaning up the breakfast things, but she could tell that Avery was trying to be reasonable. She could hear the strained patience in Avery's voice. She had to give the girl credit—she was trying.

"I'll call you tonight," Avery promised. "Yes, Mom, I love you too."

Betty was just putting the last dish in the dishwasher when Avery came back to the kitchen. "Hey, Grandma, you weren't supposed to clean up."

"It's all right." Betty smiled as she gave the speckled Formica countertop one last swipe with the sponge. "I didn't mind."

"I told my mom that I'd make a decision by tonight."

Betty just nodded.

Avery looked at her hopefully. "What do you want me to do, Grandma?"

"I want you to do what's best for you."

"But you think I need to be with my family?"

Betty pressed her lips together tightly.

"You're not going to tell me, are you?"

"I think it's a decision you need to make, Avery."

"Well, I'm not going to think about it today." Avery brightened. "Today I'm going to go decorate the church basement for the Deerwood party."

Betty blinked in surprise. "Goodness, I'd nearly forgotten that today's Friday."

"And tomorrow's the big event," Avery said. "The church secretary told me that I could come anytime after eleven today to get everything all set up for tomorrow."

Betty tried not to look too concerned. But she was feeling more than a little worried that she'd still not seen what Avery had been secretly preparing in her room. "Do I get to have a sneak peek?" she asked.

"Nope."

Betty frowned.

"Don't you trust me?"

"Yes, you know I do, Avery."

"Do you trust me to drive your car today?"

Suddenly, Betty wasn't so sure.

"I'm a good driver."

"I'm sure you are."

"And I need to load and unload everything without you seeing it," Avery continued, "or else that'll spoil the surprise. So you'll have to let me use your car, Grandma."

Just then the dog barked from outside. "You'd better let him in," Betty said, "before he wanders off."

Avery went to open the door, then came back and asked again to use the car.

"Well, I suppose I don't have much of a choice," Betty finally said.

"No, I suppose you don't." Avery grinned. "You won't be sorry."

Betty wanted to say, "I hope not," but she knew that would sound rather pessimistic. And so she just smiled and tried not to think about lime-or magenta-colored flowers. She tried not to imagine piñatas or pirates or multicolored balloons. No, she trusted Avery with this. Her granddaughter would not let her down.

"I still have some things to get ready," Avery said.

"And I have a hair appointment at nine," Betty suddenly remembered. She had booked the appointment a month ago. Going to the beauty parlor was a luxury that Betty budgeted for only twice a year. One time before Christmas and again before Easter. The rest of the time, Betty tended to her own hair. Whether it was cutting or curling it, she'd become rather adept at it over the years. Still, it always looked nicer when it was done professionally.

For nearly two blissful hours, Betty sat and listened to the hairdresser talk about everything and nothing while she worked on Betty's hair. Betty welcomed this break from thinking about runaway dogs, mixed-up granddaughters, frightening neighbors, angry daughters-in-law, and circus-like anniversary parties. And when she left the salon, she told herself that somehow everything was going to be okay. She could just feel it.

But when she got home, she found a flustered and unhappy Avery. "It's after eleven," Avery said. "And I need to get the stuff to the church."

"I know, but you can use as much time as you like to do your decor—"

"And Ralph is gone again. I checked at Jack's, but his pickup is gone too."

"Now, don't worry," Betty said. "You just go ahead and pack your things up in the car and head on over to the church. I'll find the dog, and everything will be just fine when you get back."

Avery seemed somewhat relieved, and then she smiled. "Hey, your hair looks pretty, Grandma."

Betty patted her hair. "Why, thank you."

"So, do you mind waiting in the living room while I get things loaded into the car? So that you don't see anything?"

"I'll just go and put my feet up."

"Thanks. It should only take about fifteen minutes."

"That's fine."

"And then you'll go and look for Ralph?"

Betty nodded. "I will do my best to find him."

By the time Betty heard Avery backing out of the driveway, it was close to noon. And despite being on the verge of a nap, Betty forced herself up, put on her jacket and gloves, got the dog leash, and headed out to search for the dog. She called up and down the street but didn't see the dog anywhere. And Avery was right, Jack's pickup was gone.

Betty stood on the street, looking at Jack's house and wondering if he might've possibly kidnapped the dog and then dumped him somewhere. Perhaps he'd been irked at the dog for wandering into his yard and relieving himself on the grass.

"Hey, Betty," Katie called out as she took her mail out of the box.

Betty waved and smiled. "I thought you'd have taken the girls to your mother's by now."

Katie came down the walk toward her. "That was the plan. But then my mother came down with that nasty flu, and I didn't want the girls to be exposed to it."

"I understand." Betty nodded, then frowned as she glanced over at Jack's house again. Just what was that man up to anyway? Had he taken the dog? And, if so, how would Avery react?

"Is something wrong?" Katie looked worried. "Tell me, Betty, has Jack done something again?"

Instead of voicing her concerns about Jack's interest in her granddaughter, Betty quickly explained about the missing dog.

"He's shown up at Jack's more than once, so I thought maybe he'd be there today."

"You still have that dog? I saw all those dog posters around, and I figured the owners must've called you by now."

"No." Betty shook her head. "And I'm not sure what to do about it. My granddaughter, who's staying with me right now, is getting very attached to the mutt, but we will most definitely have to find a home for him soon."

"You mean if you find him at all."

"Yes, I suppose that's true." Betty sighed. "He's a nice little dog, but he's also a bit of a nuisance with all this running-off business."

"I know what you mean." Katie pulled her knit hat down over her ears. "We had a runaway cat for a while—every time Fiona took off, the girls' hearts were just broken. I could hardly stand it. I'd waste hours on end just hunting all over for her."

"I remember," Betty said. "She was a little black and white cat. Sometimes she'd be in my yard."

Katie nodded. "We got her spayed and everything, but it made no difference. She had absolutely no sense of boundaries. She'd be gone for a week and we'd be almost ready to give up on her, then she'd come home again.

Naturally, the girls would be deliriously happy, and for a while everything would be fine. And then foolish Fiona would pull her little disappearing act again. I finally decided it was in the best interest of the girls' emotional welfare if that crazy cat was gone for good." Katie had a sly expression now. "The next time she ran away…she never came back."

Betty blinked.

"I simply took her to the pound, Betty. And I told them that the cat needed to be out on a farm where she could roam freely."

"How did the girls feel about not seeing Fiona again?"

"Naturally, they were sad. But they got over it. In the long run, it was really the kindest solution. Better to deal with these things early on—less pain that way."

Betty nodded. "That makes sense."

"Anyway, I'll let you know if I see your funny little dog around," Katie said.

Betty placed a hand on Katie's arm. "Say, I'll bet your girls would love to get a dog for Christmas."

Katie just laughed. "A runaway dog, Betty? Weren't you listening?"

"Well, I thought it was worth a try."

"Thanks anyway."

They parted ways, and Betty made a mental note to take the Gilmores a cookie plate—a small consolation for being stuck in this neighborhood during the holidays.

Betty walked up and down the street one more time, calling and looking, but with no luck. As she walked, she replayed Katie's story about the runaway Fiona. Maybe Katie was right about this. Maybe it was better to just get it over with, get rid of the dog before anyone—specifically, Avery—had time to become too attached. Yes, it made perfect sense. And if she were lucky, the dog would go away and stay away on his own. Maybe that's what he had already done. He certainly seemed the type.

She was about to turn the corner to go home and forget all about the mutt when she saw that familiar red pickup coming down the street. She waited for Jack to slow down and then watched him drive right up on the curb, over the sidewalk, and park right in the middle of his brown yard. Such a lovely sight.

"Hey," he called out to her. "I got your dog."

Betty hurried over, ready to demand to know why in the world this thoughtless young man felt it was okay to nab someone's dog and then drive him around in his truck. Furthermore, if he thought that was acceptable behavior, where did he draw the line? Would he be kidnapping Avery next and—

"I found him out in the street," Jack said as he climbed out of the pickup. The dog hopped out behind him, looking none the worse for wear. "I drove by your house earlier to drop him off, but your garage was open and your car was gone."

"I was getting my hair done." She realized that this had probably come out sounding rather snippy. But she was angry and getting angrier.

"Yeah, well, it didn't look like anyone was home. So I decided to take Ralph to the lumberyard with me."

"Ralph?" Betty was surprised that Jack actually knew the dog's name.

"Yeah, that's what Avery said she's calling him."

"Avery can call him whatever she likes, but he'll be going to the dog shelter before the day is over."

Jack scowled at her. "Shouldn't that be up to Avery?"

Betty wanted to tell him to mind his own

business but decided to go another route. "Avery will be returning to Atlanta for Christmas, and with holiday travel costs what they are these days, and this being at the last minute, I seriously doubt her parents will be willing to pay airfare for this stray dog as well." She bent down and clipped the leash onto his collar.

Jack's dark eyes felt like drills boring into her now. "Does Avery know you're taking Ralph to the pound?"

Betty blinked. "I told my granddaughter that I'd give the dog a few days to be picked up by his owners. Since that does not appear to be the case, she will surely understand about this."

Jack just pressed his lips together and shook his head.

"I am in no position to be adopting a pet," she said. Not that it was any of his business or that she needed to defend herself to the likes of him.

"I'm not suggesting you are." He just shrugged.

"Come on," she said to the dog, jerking firmly on the leash.

Jack watched her with obvious disapproval.

"Come on," she said again. Fortunately, this time the dog listened and began to move.

"Anyway," Jack called as she began to walk away, "thanks for the cookies."

She turned and looked back at him in surprise. "You...you're welcome."

Then he smiled. But, for the life of her, she could not read what was behind that smile. In some ways it seemed genuine, but the more she thought about it, the more convinced she became that it was a mocking smile. As if he knew something she didn't. And it was unnerving.

Betty took the dog into the house, put him in the laundry room, securely closed the door, and proceeded to look up the number for the animal shelter. As the phone rang, she reminded herself of Katie's story, of runaway animals and broken hearts. Really, it would be for the best.

Finally, a man answered, and she quickly explained her situation.

"We're pretty full up right now," he said.

"I'm very sorry about that," Betty said. "But this is not my dog. I've allowed him to stay with me, but I can't continue this. He had no ID or collar or anything. And it's been almost a week. I've already called the local vets and posted 'found dog' signs, and I even offered him to my neighbor as a Christmas present for her little girls."

The man chuckled. "That didn't go over?"

"Not too well." She almost told him about the runaway part but thought that might not present the dog in the best light. "So, you see," she said, "I really need to bring him in. Before the weekend, if possible."

"We're open until six."

"Thank you." Betty hung up and just hoped that Avery would get home from the church in time to make it to the shelter before six. She also hoped that Avery wouldn't be too upset or try to put the brakes on this solution. Because, really, it was for the best. It made no sense for either Betty or Avery to hang on to this mutt any longer.

And yet, if it truly was for the best, why did she feel so uncertain? Why did she feel somewhat guilty?

Just then the phone rang, causing Betty to jump.

"How are you, dear?" Marsha asked.

"Oh my! Do you really want to know?"

"Of course I do. What's the matter?"

So Betty poured out the whole frustrating story about the stray dog and the unexpected granddaughter and everything. Almost. The only part she left out was in regard to Jack. But that was only because she knew Marsha lived a protected life. With a gated neighborhood and a modern security system in her home, Marsha couldn't possibly understand a neighbor like Jack.

"Is there anything I can do for you?"

"As a matter of fact, yes." Betty told her about the need to take the dog to the shelter. "I'd drive him myself, but I let Avery use my car so she could set things up for your anniversary party tomorrow."

"Avery is setting things up?"

Betty could hear the concern in Marsha's voice. "Oh, she's very talented," Betty said. "Much more creative than I am."

"Really?"

"She's been working on it for the past few days."

"The past few days?" Now Marsha sounded impressed, and Betty worried that she may have overstated things. "Isn't that nice."

"So, you see, I'm without a car. And I'm worried the shelter may close before Avery gets back. And then we'd be stuck with the dog all weekend, and I just don't know what to—"

"Well, I was just on my way out to pick up Jim's favorite suit at the cleaner's. How about if I come and pick you up?"

"Oh, I would be so grateful, Marsha. You're sure you don't mind?"

"What are friends for?"

Betty waited on pins and needles, watching eagerly for Marsha's silver Cadillac to pull up. She so wanted to take care of this business before Avery got back from the church. She'd already put on her coat, and the dog was on his leash. Her purse and gloves were ready to grab up in order to make her getaway.

It was nearly two when she saw Marsha's car coming down her street, and even before she pulled into the driveway, Betty and Ralph were out the door and heading toward her.

"My, but you are eager," Marsha said as Betty opened the door on the passenger side.

"I didn't want to waste any of your time."

Marsha frowned slightly. "I don't suppose you have a doggy carrier for him, do you?"

"I'm sorry." Betty bent down to pick up the dog, then eased herself backward onto the seat and planted the dog securely on her lap before turning her legs around. "But I'm sure he'll be no trouble."

"I just don't want him to scratch the leather upholstery. Jim wouldn't appreciate that."

"I'll be very careful."

"Very wise of you to take care of this doggy business before the holidays," Marsha said. "Pets can be such a nuisance, underfoot, breaking things."

Betty felt unexpectedly defensive of the little dog just then. And she almost told Marsha that this animal was different, that he didn't break things or get underfoot, and he certainly would not scratch up Marsha's upholstery. At least she hoped not. And he didn't disappoint her—he sat perfectly quiet as Marsha drove them across town.

"I'm so looking forward to the celebration tomorrow," Marsha said. "I can't wait to see who comes." She explained that her daughter Karen had let it slip that they'd received some unexpected RSVPs. "She wouldn't say specifically from whom, but I could tell by the way Karen said it that we'd be pleasantly surprised."

"How nice." Betty patted the dog on the head and tried not to feel guilty for what she was about to do. Surely the dog would find a good home. Besides, what choice did she have? Avery would be returning to Atlanta soon. Having the dog around would only make it harder on everyone. Betty was doing her granddaughter a favor. Not only would it please Avery's parents, but it would keep her out of harm's way where Jack was concerned.

"Here we are," Marsha said as she pulled up to a cinderblock structure that looked more like a prison than a shelter. "Would you like me to come in with you?"

Betty considered this. The truth was that moral support would be most welcome right now. But then she looked at Marsha's lovely leather jacket and considered the animal smells that would most likely permeate the building, combined with Marsha's general disapproval of pets. "No," she finally said. "I'll be fine. But thanks for offering."

Betty picked up the dog and set him outside the car, but she could tell by his quivering body that he was just as nervous as she. And he was probably even more frightened. Still, she suppressed these troublesome thoughts as she walked toward the entrance. This really was in the best interest of everyone, she told herself as she reached for the door. Katie had said as much, and so had Marsha. Betty was foolish to think otherwise.

As she entered the building, hearing barks

and yelps of other dogs, she knew that she'd done Avery a big favor by handling this on her own. It took strength to do something like this.

"May I help you?" asked a young woman in blue jeans and a sweatshirt.

Betty quickly explained her phone call and how a man had told her she could bring the dog in. The woman asked her some questions and finally handed her a rather lengthy form. Betty carefully filled it in and gave it back to her.

The woman studied the form, then frowned at Betty. "You're sure you wouldn't want to keep this dog?"

Betty glanced down at the dog. He looked up with such trusting brown eyes that she forced herself to turn away. She shook her head. "No, no. I can't have a dog. You see, I go to Florida next month, and I don't have anyone to care for him…" She continued rambling about how she planned to sell her house and perhaps look into some kind of retirement home. Even to her own ears it all sounded rather lonely and sad…and perhaps a little bit phony.

The woman took the leash from Betty's hand. "It's not required, but we like to recommend that people who leave pets in the shelter make some kind of a donation toward the welfare of the animal."

Betty tried not to look too surprised as she opened her purse. "I live on a fixed income," she explained as she extracted a ten-dollar bill and several ones. "Will this be enough?"

"Thank you." The woman smiled. "That will help to buy pet food."

Betty nodded and backed away from the woman and the dog. "Yes…I suppose it will." She turned and made her way to the front door, realizing that everything looked blurry now. She reached for the doorknob but couldn't actually see it. She fumbled until it turned in her hand. Then, as she went out into the cold air, she realized she had tears running down her cheeks. She was crying again. The third time this week. And this time, she was crying harder.

She paused to reach for a handkerchief, drying her tears and blowing her nose before getting back into Marsha's warm car. *Goodness*, she thought as she tucked her hanky back in her coat pocket, *all this emotion— just for a dog?*

Chapter Eleven

Betty was relieved to see that her car was not in the garage when Marsha pulled into her driveway.

"You seem very quiet today," Marsha said as she put her car into park. "Are you sure you're okay?"

Betty sniffed. "As I said, it's been a little stressful this week."

"I hope our anniversary party hasn't added to your stress."

"No, not at all. In fact, Avery seems to have thoroughly enjoyed helping."

"I'm so excited to see what she's done."

Betty nodded. "So am I."

"And now I better get over to the cleaner's." Marsha looked at her watch. "Can you believe that I'm still not finished packing yet?"

"Oh, I nearly forgot about the cruise Jim

booked." Betty gathered her purse and reached for the door handle. "When do you leave again?"

"Sunday morning. We'll miss the Christmas service in church."

"I'll miss you too." Betty sighed as she opened the door.

"At least you'll have Avery to keep you company." Marsha reached over and patted Betty's shoulder. "That's a real comfort to me. I told Jim that I felt sad to think of you spending Christmas alone this year."

Betty forced a smile. She did not intend to tell Marsha that Avery might be going home after all. Why cause her concern? "Avery has decorated the house and wants us to cook a turkey. Do you know I haven't cooked a turkey in years?" Betty was out of the car now. "I'll see you tomorrow, Marsha. Thank you again for helping me with the dog."

Marsha waved as she backed out of the driveway.

Betty went through the garage into the house. She paused by the laundry room, where the dog's things were still in their place, as if the dog would be coming home any moment. Betty quickly gathered up the dog bed and bowls and stashed them on a low shelf in the garage. Out of sight, out of mind. Or so she hoped.

Then she made a cup of tea and sat down in her recliner to relax. But as she sat there, all she could think about was that silly little dog. And even when she closed her eyes, hoping for a nap, she felt as if those liquid-brown canine eyes were indelibly printed inside her head. Finally, she reached for the remote and turned on the TV, flipping through the familiar channels until a figure skater appeared.

"I'm home," Avery called as she came into the living room.

Betty opened her eyes, blinking into the light.

"Sorry, Grandma. Did I wake you?"

"It's okay." She smiled at her granddaughter, watching as Avery removed her parka and unwound the bright scarf from around her neck.

"It's so cold out." Avery rubbed her hands together. "I really think it's going to snow."

"You might be right." Betty put the footrest down and sat up straight. "So, tell me, how did the decorating go?"

Avery's eyes lit up. "It was awesome, Grandma. It looks really, really cool."

"Cool?" Betty nodded, taking this in.

"Way better than I expected. No one will even remember they're in the church basement. It's like another world down there now."

"Another world?" Betty wasn't sure what to make of that. Was it another world like Mexico, or a pirate's cove, or Mars perhaps? Still, she was determined not to show the slightest sign of distrust.

"Where's Ralph?" Avery asked.

Betty stood slowly.

"Grandma?" Avery's voice sounded worried now. "Where is he? Did you find him? Is he okay?"

"Avery…" Betty looked into her granddaughter's eyes. "I have something to tell you."

"Has he been hurt?" Avery looked truly upset now.

"No, he's perfectly fine."

Avery looked relieved. "Oh, good. But where is he? Outside?"

"He's not here."

Avery frowned. "Where is he, Grandma?"

Betty walked into the kitchen. She knew she was stalling, but she just hadn't thought this through properly. How was she going to explain to Avery what she'd done? How was she going to make her understand?

"Grandma?" Avery followed her.

"The dog had run away again," Betty began. "I looked all over the neighborhood for him, Avery. I was quite worried. Finally, I found him. It turned out he was with Jack, in his truck."

"Did Jack take Ralph?"

"No."

"Then what?" Avery said. "Where is Ralph?"

"I knew that you were considering going home for Christmas, Avery. In fact, I think that's probably just what you need to do, and—"

"What does that have to do with Ralph?"

"Well, as you know, I can't keep a dog. I'll be going to Susan's in January. And I may even sell my—"

"Please, Grandma, just cut to the chase. Where is Ralph?"

"I took him to the animal shelter."

"To the pound? You took him to the pound?"

"It's an animal shelter," Betty corrected. "They'll take good care of him and find him a home or perhaps his original own—"

"Unless the pound is overcrowded," Avery snapped. "And then they might just kill him."

"Oh, no," Betty said quickly. "They are

good people. And I gave them money for dog food. They won't hurt him." But even as she said this, she didn't know it for certain. And the idea of those people hurting that dog, or that Betty was responsible, cut through her like a knife.

Avery was crying now. She sank down into a kitchen chair, holding her head in her hands and sobbing. "I love that dog, Grandma. I needed him."

Betty didn't know what to say. And when the phone rang, she was relieved for the distraction. Until she realized it was Avery's mother on the other end. She'd completely forgotten about Avery's promise to make a decision by tonight.

"Hello, Stephanie." Betty's voice was flat.

"May I speak to Avery, please?"

Betty glanced to where Avery was still sobbing at the kitchen table. "Avery is, uh, well, she's unable to come to the phone right now."

"Unable? Or unwilling?"

"She's a bit upset," Betty said.

"Upset? Why? What's going on there, Betty?"

"She's sad that I took a stray dog to the animal shelter."

"Is that all? Well, put her on the line, please. I need to speak to her."

Betty stretched the cord of the phone over to where Avery was sitting. Covering the mouthpiece, Betty said quietly, "It's your mother, dear. She wants to speak to you."

Avery looked up with watery eyes. "I don't want to speak to her." Then she stood, but before she left the room, she added, "Or you either."

Betty felt a lump in her throat as she put the phone back to her ear. "I'm sorry, Stephanie, but Avery really doesn't want to talk right now."

"Well, when does Avery want to talk?"

"I really can't say, dear." Betty heard the front door open and close.

"Because we need to figure this out. Gary just found an airline ticket online. It's not cheap, but it's better than we expected."

"That's good."

"That's only good if Avery is coming home."

"Yes, that's true." Betty looked out the kitchen window, peering out into the darkness and worrying about her granddaughter being out on the streets alone on a cold winter night.

"And we don't know if Avery is coming home. There is no point in wasting good money on air fare if Avery has no intention of coming home. Do you understand what I'm saying to you, Betty?" Stephanie said as if she were speaking to a child.

"Of course."

"So, can you tell me what we should do? Should I tell Gary to get the ticket?"

"I really don't know."

"Can you promise me that you'll see to it that Avery gets to the airport and gets on the plane? It's a red-eye flight."

"A red-eye flight?"

"Yes. The plane leaves at 10:15 p.m. your time."

"At night?"

"P.m. means night, Betty."

"Yes, I know that." She imagined herself driving Avery to the airport at night. Betty did not see well after dark. And the airport was nearly an hour away.

"So, do we book the flight or not, Betty?" Stephanie's voice was sounding more and more impatient. She reminded Betty of a rubber band that was stretched too tightly.

"I just don't see how I can possibly make that decision," Betty said.

"Well, someone needs to."

"And I believe that someone is Avery."

"Then put Avery on the phone!"

"I can't."

"Why not?"

"Because she's not here."

"But you said—"

"She stepped out."

"But it's nighttime. Even in your time zone it must be dark out."

"Yes, it is. I'm sorry, Stephanie, but I really don't see how I can help you. You and Gary will have to make your own decision about the plane ticket."

Somehow Betty managed to extract herself from the phone conversation, then she hurriedly put on her coat and went outside to see if she could find Avery. She went up and down the street, looking this way and that, feeling foolish, old, and tired. Really, what chance did she have of catching up with a young girl?

Finally, she returned home in defeat. Out of curiosity, she checked Avery's room. It was something of a relief to see that Avery had taken nothing with her. Not even her purse. Perhaps she was just taking a walk to cool off. But with temperatures dropping below freezing tonight, she would cool off quickly.

It was nearly eight when Betty finally made some oatmeal for her dinner, but even then she didn't feel hungry. Where was Avery? Was she okay? Should Betty call the police and report her as missing? Would they even be concerned? Wasn't there some kind of rule about a person being missing more than one day before they would search? But perhaps Betty could explain that her granddaughter was distraught, possibly even depressed. Would they go and look for her then? If Marsha and Jim weren't busy packing and preparing for their big day tomorrow as well as their anniversary cruise, Betty would call them and ask for help.

After only a few bites, Betty dumped her oatmeal and began to clean the kitchen. By nine, she decided to call the local police. Really, what could it hurt? But as she expected, they did not want to file a missing persons report yet.

"Most cases like this resolve themselves," the woman told her. "Your granddaughter is probably on her way home right now."

"But—"

"If it makes you feel better, I'll let our patrolmen know that she's out there."

"Oh, yes, I would appreciate that." Betty gave her a description of Avery, thanked her again, and hung up. She looked out the living room window, staring out into the darkened street and hoping that, like the policewoman had assured her, Avery would suddenly show up at the door.

Finally, Betty attempted to watch some TV. And eventually she just went to bed, but she was too worried to sleep. And so she prayed. She prayed that somehow God would unravel this tangled mess that she felt responsible for creating. She prayed that God would somehow take what appeared to be evil and transform it into good.

At just a few minutes past eleven, Betty heard the front door open and close. She'd purposely left it unlocked in the hopes that Avery would return. But now she was worried. What if a perfect stranger had just walked into her home? Perhaps her strange neighbor Jack?

Betty remained motionless, almost afraid to breathe as she listened to quiet footsteps. Then she heard someone using the bathroom. And then going into Avery's room and closing the door. Of course, it had to be Avery. But just to be sure, Betty slipped out of bed and tiptoed to the living room. Hanging limply over the back of an armchair was Avery's parka and bright red scarf. She was safe.

Chapter Twelve

Betty slept in later than usual on Saturday morning. Probably due to her late night and worries about her granddaughter. Still, she felt hopeful as she got out of bed. She was optimistic as she did her morning stretches, then pulled on her thick, quilted robe. Avery was home, and this morning they would talk. Betty would apologize for taking Ralph (yes, she was calling the dog by his name now) to the shelter. And perhaps she and Avery could figure this whole thing out together. Maybe there was a way that Avery could keep the dog. Even if it meant Betty had to use some of her savings to pay for the dog to fly to Atlanta with Avery. Oh, some might think it foolish on Betty's part, but maybe it was just what the girl needed.

Avery's bedroom door was open, but Avery was not in her room. Her bed was neatly made, and some of her clothes were folded and sitting at the foot of it.

"Avery?" Betty tapped lightly on the partially opened bathroom door. But Avery wasn't in there. Betty continued to look through the house, only to discover that Avery wasn't there at all. But where could she be? Suddenly Betty realized that she'd never gotten her car keys back from Avery last night. But when she hurried out to the garage, she found the car parked there as usual.

As Betty made coffee—a full pot since she told herself that Avery had simply taken a morning stroll—the phone rang again. This time it was Gary, and all Betty could tell him was that Avery had come home safely last night but had gone out again this morning.

"This isn't helpful, Mother."

"I'm sorry, but that's all I know."

"Steph is really bugging me to get that ticket."

"Like I told her yesterday, that is up to you. I don't know how to advise you."

"Well, when Avery comes in, please ask her to call."

She promised to do that and hung up. A

part of her was tempted to jerk the cord out of the wall, but she knew that wasn't a very responsible thing to do. Instead, she sat down and drank her coffee and prayed that Avery would come home soon. Surely she'd want to go to Jim and Marsha's anniversary celebration this afternoon. She had worked so hard on those decorations and had been so excited about everything. Betty remembered how her face had lit up while she was talking about it yesterday. Yes, Avery would certainly want to go to the party.

But at one twenty, Avery was still not back. The party was supposed to start at two, but Betty had planned to get there early to check on things. So she left Avery a note along with bus fare, saying that she looked forward to seeing her at the celebration.

Betty grew increasingly nervous as she drove toward the church. Suddenly she was remembering those gaudy flowers again, those mysterious bags, and how Avery had holed up in her room. What if she'd actually created a monstrosity? What if Avery was too embarrassed to show her face at the church now? How would Betty explain it? How could she possibly apologize or make it up to her good friends?

Betty parked in the back, thankful that no other cars were there yet. It was barely one thirty now. If the decorations were truly a disaster, Betty might have enough time to make changes, to cover up for her granddaughter's lack of discretion.

She entered the church and headed straight down the stairs, bracing herself. She was about to turn on the lights when she realized there was already some light down there. Not bright, but enough to see.

Betty entered the room and was stunned to find that the basement had been transformed into a gold and white fairyland. So pretty it literally took her breath away. How was it possible that Avery had done this? And on such a frugal budget? It seemed nothing short of miraculous.

Betty walked through the room, admiring a concoction of gauzy white fabric that was hung like an arbor over the main table. The folds of fabric were sprinkled with gold sparkles and tiny stars and intertwined with small white Christmas lights. There were pearly white and gold balloons here and there, and an abundance of gold and white flowers artfully arranged. Upon closer investigation, Betty discovered that spray paint had been involved—Avery had used metallic gold and white spray paint to transform the previously bright-colored artificial blooms into something much more dignified and fitting for a golden anniversary.

Paper doilies were painted gold, arranged beautifully beneath small stacks of white paper plates and embossed napkins. If Avery had told Betty she was using plain paper plates, Betty would've been concerned. But the way Avery had placed and arranged everything—it was all perfectly elegant. It was truly a work of art. Betty wished she'd thought to bring a camera. But surely someone would have one.

Now Betty noticed a number of white candles that had touches of gold spray paint, like gilt, to make them lovelier. And nearby was a box of matches and what appeared to be a folded note with "Betty Kowalski" written on it.

Dear Grandma,

I came by and turned the light strings on. All you need to do is light the candles and it should be all set for Jim and Marsha. I'm sorry to miss it. And I'm sorry I've been so much trouble for you.

I know I need to figure out my own life, and that's what I plan to do. Thank you for putting up with me.
Love,
Avery

Betty refolded the note and slipped it into her purse. Avery must've stopped by here sometime earlier. Perhaps just to make sure that everything was still okay. But why hadn't she stayed for the party? What difference would a few more hours make? Why had Avery been in such a hurry?

Of course, Betty knew why. It was because of her…and what she'd done to Ralph.

Betty put her coat and purse in the closet and slowly went about the room, lighting the various candles and pausing to admire the beauty of her granddaughter's handiwork. The flickering candlelight, which was reflected on surfaces of metallic gold, made the room even more magical than it had been before. It was a masterpiece. And Betty knew that Marsha and Jim would appreciate it.

As she stood off to one side, looking at the scene from a distance, she realized that once again she was crying. She went into the bathroom, blew her nose, and dried her tears, telling herself that she was too old for such melodrama.

And, really, shouldn't she be happy for her granddaughter? Avery's note had actually sounded very mature. As if she had finally decided to take responsibility for her own life. To stand on her own two feet. Yet Betty couldn't help but wonder how Avery would accomplish this with little or no money. How could Avery possibly take care of herself? What would she eat? Where would she sleep? How would she manage to get by?

Betty heard some young-sounding voices outside of the bathroom and suddenly felt hopeful. Perhaps Avery had changed her mind and come back. Maybe she'd give Betty a chance to start over again after all. Eagerly, Betty went out into the room to discover Jim and Marsha and their children and grandchildren. They were going around the room oohing and aahing, obviously pleased with Avery's creation. Betty forced a smile to cover her disappointment as she said, "Happy anniversary!"

"Oh, Betty," Marsha gushed, "it's so beautiful!"

"Did you do this?" asked Marsha's younger daughter, Lynn.

"No, not me," Betty said quickly.

"It was Betty's granddaughter, Avery," Marsha said.

"Well, it's incredible," Lynn said.

"Is your granddaughter an artist?" one of the grandchildren asked. Betty didn't recall the little girl's name.

Betty nodded proudly. "Yes, I think she is."

"Is she here?" she asked eagerly.

Betty sighed. "No, unfortunately, she had to leave."

"I want to get photos of this before anything gets messed up," Lynn said. "Mom and Dad, you go stand over there beneath that arbor thing, and let's get some shots."

Soon the cake arrived, and although Betty wasn't on the refreshment committee or the cleanup committee, she spent most of her time helping in the kitchen. Oh, she made an appearance now and then, smiling and visiting congenially, but mostly she wanted to remain behind the scenes, alone with her thoughts. She didn't wish to spoil her friends' fun, so she hid her broken heart behind busyness.

Finally, the party was winding down. Jim and Marsha came into the kitchen and thanked Betty again. "It was so beautiful,"

Marsha said. "I wish Avery had been able to come. I would've loved to tell her in person how brilliant I think she is."

"I'm sure Betty will pass that along," Jim said.

"Of course." Betty nodded.

"Will you join us for dinner?" Marsha asked. "Lynn surprised us by having it all catered at our house, and I know there's plenty for—"

"No thank you," Betty said quickly.

"Avery could come too," Jim said.

"Thanks, but we have other plans."

"Are you sure?" Marsha looked disappointed.

"Yes." Betty forced a smile.

Then Marsha and Jim hugged Betty and wished both her and Avery a merry Christmas. Betty told them to have a delightful cruise and to send a postcard.

"Count on it," Marsha said as she rejoined her family.

Betty remained in the kitchen just puttering around, wiping things that she'd already wiped, and waiting for everyone to depart on their merry ways. Finally, it was only the cleanup committee that remained, and they were getting right to work.

"Hey, Betty," Irene called out, "do you want to save any of these decorations?"

Betty went out and looked around the room. It no longer seemed magical with the harsh glare from the florescent overhead lights. Irene blew the last candle out, and others gathered up trash, plates with remnants of uneaten cake, plastic cups, and wadded-up napkins.

She was about to say no but then thought of Avery and all her hard work. She went to the main table and picked up a candle that was wreathed in gold and white flowers. "Yes," she told Irene. "I'll keep this as a memento."

"We'll put some of these other things in the wedding closet," Irene said. "You never know what might come in handy."

Betty nodded. "You never know." Then she got her coat and purse and went out to her car. It was just getting dusky out, and as Betty drove, she couldn't help but keep a lookout for Avery. How she longed to spot the girl, to pick her up, hug her tightly, and take her home. But there was no sign of her.

As Betty turned down her street, she saw that it was beginning to snow. Perhaps Avery's much-longed-for white Christmas was about to become a reality. But where was Avery?

Suddenly, Betty grew hopeful again. Perhaps Avery was at home. Maybe she'd realized that being broke and homeless on a cold day like this was not all she'd hoped it would be. Maybe she'd come to her senses.

Betty was tempted to drive fast, but she knew the streets were getting slick, and her night vision was lacking, so she went slowly and carefully. But when she got into the house, it looked just as it had when she'd left. Avery's clothes were still folded neatly at the foot of her bed. This had given Betty some hope earlier, thinking that Avery had probably planned to return. But as Betty looked more closely, it seemed that most of Avery's things, including her oversized bag and personal items from the bathroom, were missing. As if she had packed up and left for good. Those few items of clothing still on the bed had probably been too bulky to stuff into her bag.

Betty picked up a wooly sweater that Avery had purchased for two dollars at Goodwill, and held it to her chest. Why hadn't Avery taken this with her? If it was too big to pack, she could've at least worn it under her parka.

It would've been much warmer than some of those other lightweight blouses Avery often wore. Why hadn't she taken it with her? And why had she left at all?

Chapter Thirteen

At five thirty, Betty put together a cookie platter for the Gilmores. She'd been meaning to do this for a couple of days, but what with Avery, the dog, and the anniversary party, she had forgotten. But now, despite the weather and the hour, she was determined to get it delivered. And her determination was twofold. Naturally, she wanted to be neighborly. But she also wanted to know if, by any chance, they had observed Avery coming or going today. Perhaps Katie had spoken to her. Although it seemed unlikely.

There was a dusting of snow on the sidewalk as Betty made her way down the street, then knocked on the Gilmores' door.

"Oh!" Katie opened the door, holding a roll

of Santa wrapping paper in her hand. "What are you doing out in this weather?"

Betty forced a smile. "Wishing my neighbors a merry Christmas!" She held out the cookie tray.

"Oh, thank you!" Katie stuck the roll of wrapping paper beneath her elbow to receive the platter of sweets. "Won't you come in?"

"Perhaps for a minute."

"Martin took the girls out to get a Christmas tree," Katie said as Betty came inside. "He grew up in a family that firmly believed respectable people never put up their trees *until* Christmas Eve. But the girls begged and begged, and he finally gave in. So this year our tree will be up two days before Christmas." She winked. "That's progress."

"Yes." Betty nodded and smiled.

Katie cleared away wrapping paper and ribbons to make a spot for the cookies on the dining room table. "Would you like some coffee or tea or—"

"No thank you. I really can't stay. I can see you're busy."

"And I know you have your granddaughter visiting…" Katie frowned slightly, as if something unpleasant just occurred to her.

"Yes? What about my granddaughter?" Betty leaned forward. "Have you seen her today?"

"I realize it's not really any of my business."

"What isn't your business?"

"Well, I did notice your granddaughter today. I was picking up the newspaper this morning, and I saw her."

Betty nodded. "And?"

"And…I couldn't help but notice she was with Jack."

"Oh?"

"Yes. I thought it was rather odd, Betty. I hadn't imagined that they'd be friends."

"Well, Avery has met Jack. And they actually had a nice little chat the other day. It seems he's lonely, and it's the holidays, and…" Betty didn't know what else to say. And despite her reassuring words, her heart was beginning to pound.

"Oh. Well, it just caught my attention to see her with him. They were getting into his truck."

"Jack's pickup?" For some reason, this struck Betty as strange. It was one thing to visit with a neighbor, something else altogether to let them take you somewhere in their vehicle.

Katie nodded. "Yes. And...I don't know how to say this, except to just spit it out in the open."

"Say what?"

"Your granddaughter seemed, uh, a little upset."

"Was Jack forcing her into his pickup?"

"I don't think so. But something about the whole thing just struck me wrong—I felt worried."

"Oh dear!" Betty's hand flew to her mouth.

"I'm sorry, Betty. I had meant to mention it to you earlier, just to make sure everything was okay. But then things got hectic, and Martin offered to watch the girls so I could do some last-minute Christmas shopping, and by the time I got back, you were gone. I got busy wrapping presents, and I guess I just forgot."

A rush of panic jolted through Betty. What if Avery, after a short conversation, had trusted Jack? And what if he'd turned out to be just the sort of person that Betty and everyone else in the neighborhood had feared? What if he had somehow tricked Avery? What if she was in trouble now?

"So, is everything okay? I mean with your granddaughter?"

"Actually…she's missing."

Katie's eyes grew wide. "Oh no! I'm so sorry, Betty. I knew I should've said something sooner."

"I'm sure everything is fine." But Betty could hear the tremor in her voice.

"Where do you think she is?"

Betty considered this. "I don't really know. But I know who I'm going to ask."

"Jack?" Katie looked slightly horrified.

"Yes."

"Oh, Betty, don't go over there alone. Not at night."

"I need to speak to him."

"Why don't you wait for Martin to get home? I'm sure he'd go over there with you."

"No, this can't wait." Betty's hand was on the door now.

"You can't go alone." Katie reached for her jacket. "I'm coming too."

"No, Katie." Betty shook her head. "You stay here."

"I can't. But wait and let me get my cell phone. I'll be ready to call 911 if it's necessary."

Betty decided not to argue, and they walked

over to Jack's house. His pickup was there, and the lights were on inside the house.

"I'll knock on the door," Betty said.

"What if he doesn't answer?"

"I'll make him answer."

"I'm scared."

"You stay back," Betty said. "If anything goes awry, you make a run for it and call the police."

Katie just nodded. Her face looked pale in the streetlight.

Betty turned, took a deep breath, and marched up to Jack's door. First she rang the doorbell several times, then she pounded loudly with her fist. Suddenly the door opened, and she nearly struck Jack in the chest with her final blow.

"What's going on?" he said.

Betty stepped back, then remembered her mission. "I'm looking for my granddaughter," she said.

"She's not here."

"But you were seen with her. You took her somewhere in your truck this morning."

He shrugged. "Yeah, I gave her a ride."

"But she's missing." Betty stared at him, trying to see if there was evil in his countenance.

"Missing?" He looked slightly confused now.

"Yes. She never came home."

He nodded as if he knew something. "Of course not."

"What do you mean by that?"

"She didn't come home because I took her to the bus station."

"The bus station?"

"Look." He rubbed his hands on his bare arms. "It's cold out here. Why don't you come inside and we can discuss this calmly?"

Betty glanced over her shoulder to Katie, who was now standing directly behind her on the porch.

"You can both come in," he said.

"Fine," Katie said. "But first I'm calling Martin to let him know where I'm at."

They waited for Katie to make her call, and then the two women followed Jack into his house. He took them past the foyer and into what had once been a formal living room, but because some walls had been removed, it now seemed to be part of the kitchen, and it was also connected to the small family room and dining room. Instead of four rooms, it was now simply one. Did he plan to knock out all the walls and turn the house into a big barn?

"You've made some changes," Betty said.

"Wow," Katie said as she looked around.

"This is exactly what I've been telling Martin that I want to do with our house. Have a great room."

"A great room?" Betty was confused. "It looks like a great big mess to me."

"No," Katie said. "It's opened up so that a family can be together in one space."

"That's right." Jack nodded toward a couple of folding lawn chairs. "I don't have much furniture, but you're welcome to sit down if you like."

"No thank you." Betty turned her attention back to Jack. "Let's cut right to the chase, Jack. What have you done with my granddaughter?"

"Like I said, I dropped her at the bus station. Well, that was after I took her by a church."

"A church?"

"She needed to leave a note with somebody."

Betty nodded. "And after that you took her to the bus station?"

"That's what I just told you."

"What time was it then?"

His brow creased. "I'm not sure. But it wasn't noon yet. Maybe not even eleven. Avery had come over to my place fairly early."

"She came to your house?" Katie asked.

"Yeah. We'd arranged to meet here in the morning."

"You *arranged* to meet her?" Betty frowned. "Why?"

"She wanted my help."

"Why?" Katie asked.

"Because she'd been over the night before. She was upset about losing the dog. We spent a long time talking things out. She decided that it was time for her to move on with her life, so she asked me to help her."

"To help her?" Betty said.

Jack shoved his hands in his jeans pockets but didn't answer.

"How exactly did you plan to help her?" Betty persisted.

"She was broke. She wanted to get away from here." He scowled at Betty. "And she wanted to get away from you too. She wasn't too pleased with what you did to her dog."

Betty felt her cheeks flush. "Yes, I know."

He shook his finger at her. "She really loved that dog."

Katie looked at Betty with an alarmed expression. "What did you do to the dog?"

"I took him to the animal shelter."

"Oh, well…" Katie shrugged. "That was probably for the best."

"Unless you're attached to the animal and want to keep it," Jack shot back at her. "Avery didn't even have a say in the matter. That wasn't fair."

"I know." Betty nodded again. "Jack's right about that. I regret what I did."

"You do?" Jack looked surprised.

"Yes, I do. But back to Avery. You say you took her to the bus station. Do you know where she was going?"

He shook his head. "I assumed she was going home, to her family."

Betty felt a small wave of relief. And yet she wasn't sure. How could she trust Jack? What if he'd concocted this whole story, and in the meantime, Avery was tied and gagged back there in one of the bedrooms?

Betty frowned. "Do you mind if I use your restroom?"

He gave her a funny look. "Seriously?"

"If it's okay with you."

"Well, the powder room is torn out right now."

"I know." Betty nodded toward the backyard. "I've been privileged to enjoy the pink commode with my morning coffee."

He kind of chuckled. "Sorry about that. I guess it's time to make a run to the dump again."

"I know where the other bathroom is," she told him as she headed down the hallway. Fortunately, the doors to the first two bedrooms were open. Except for some random boxes and building things, the rooms appeared to be empty. Betty paused by the master bedroom and was relieved to see that, except for a mattress topped with a sleeping bag in the center of the floor, it too appeared vacant. And since all the closet doors had been removed, there was no place else to hide a captive.

She went into the bathroom, which was surprisingly neat considering the state of the rest of the house, and after a few seconds, she flushed the toilet. Then, satisfied that Avery was not in the house, she returned to find Jack and Katie discussing, of all things, remodeling.

"The trick is not to change the plumbing and electrical," he was explaining to Katie. "That helps to keep costs down." He eyed Betty. "Did you have a good look around?"

Betty just cleared her throat. "Did you stay

at the bus station to make sure Avery got onto the bus safely?"

He frowned. "She's not a baby. I'm pretty sure she knows how to take care of herself."

"But did she have enough money for the fare?" Betty frowned. "Atlanta is a long way."

"She had enough fare money as well as money for food."

Betty felt her shoulders relax. "I really should thank you, Jack."

"No problem."

"And I'd like to pay you back."

"Avery promised to pay me back."

"Well, okay. Then I suppose we should go. I need to let her parents know that she's on her way."

"Don't you think Avery would have done that by now?" he asked.

"Perhaps, but they've been quite worried."

He nodded. "I guess you'd know best, Mrs. Kowalski."

Betty was suddenly seeing this young man in a new light. Why had she been so hard on him before? So suspicious?

She stuck out her hand. "Just call me Betty, please." As they shook, it occurred to her that, like her, Jack had some challenges. She also knew, better than some, how challenges sometimes led to grumpiness. Maybe everyone just needed to be a little more patient, a little more understanding. After all, wasn't it almost Christmas?

He released her hand and smiled. "Just call me Jack." His face was transformed by that smile. And for the first time, she realized that he was fairly attractive in a rugged sort of way. "Oh, yeah." He chuckled. "You already do call me Jack."

"Sorry to have bothered you," she said.

"It's okay."

"Thanks for the remodeling tips," Katie said as they went to the door.

"And thanks for the cookies, Betty," Jack called out. "They were great."

She turned and smiled at him. "I have more, if you'd like some."

He looked away and sort of shrugged, and suddenly she wondered if she'd stepped over some kind of invisible line again. "Thanks again," she said anyway. "I mean for helping Avery like you did."

Betty and Katie walked down the sidewalk until Katie finally spoke. "He seems kind of nice."

"Yes…perhaps we were wrong about him all along."

"Unless he's very good at covering something up." Katie lowered her voice. "I've read about serial killers, Betty, and some of them seem very nice on the surface. But they're actually coldhearted, psychopath murderers underneath."

Betty stopped walking and turned to face Katie. "Do you really think that Jack is a psychopath?"

"I honestly don't know…and I'll admit that sometimes I have an overactive imagination."

Betty shivered in the cold.

"But that's the problem with psychopaths, Betty. Most of the time people don't figure it out until it's too late."

Betty just shook her head and continued walking. Maybe it was a mistake to listen to Katie. After all, she was nearly a third Betty's age. What made her such an expert on anything?

"I'm sorry." Katie put a hand on Betty's shoulder as they paused by the Gilmores' house. "I'm sure Jack's not a psychopath serial killer. Like Martin says, I should quit reading those horrible books."

"Perhaps so…" Betty told Katie thank you and good night and hurried back to her own house, carefully locking the doors and the deadbolts once she was inside. She shuddered to think that she'd gone to bed with her front door unlocked last night. But that had been for Avery's sake. Surely there was no chance she'd try to slip in late tonight.

Betty still felt unsettled as she picked up the phone to call her son and daughter-in-law. But she was determined to remain calm and collected. Thankfully, it was Gary who answered, and she quickly told him what she'd just learned about Avery. Hopefully, it was the truth and not a cover-up.

"I can't tell you exactly when she'll get there," she said. "But the neighbor who told me made it sound as if she was heading your way."

"Well, that's a relief. That airline ticket didn't last long online, and I doubt that we'll find another one in time for Christmas now."

"So perhaps it's for the best."

"Maybe so. Thanks, Mom."

Betty controlled the urge to apologize. She longed to confess all and to tell her son that this foolish mess was all her fault. She wanted to admit how she'd failed Avery, how she'd betrayed her trust. But she suspected that would only make him feel more concerned for Avery's welfare. Better to wait until Avery was safely home, and then Betty would gladly take the blame. And hopefully, Avery would forgive her.

"I'll go online tonight and check the bus schedules from your town so we can have an idea of when to look for her," Gary said. "And we'll be sure to let you know when she arrives."

"Thanks, I appreciate that." But after they said good-bye, more doubts began to creep into Betty's frazzled mind. As much as she wanted to trust Jack, to believe what he had told her, how could she be certain? What if, like Katie had suggested, he really was a psychopath skilled at telling people what he thought they wanted to hear? What if Avery was actually in danger?

Once again, Betty knew her only answer, her only recourse, her only real lifeline, was to pray. And so she would pray and hope for the best.

Chapter Fourteen

Betty got up early on Sunday. But as she walked through her house, going through the paces of pulling on her old robe, slipping into her worn slippers, and putting on coffee, she felt more alone than ever. She looked at the Christmas decorations Avery had placed around the house. So jolly and festive just days ago, they seemed to be mocking her now. Who was she to expect a merry Christmas?

Betty looked out her kitchen window as she sipped her coffee. A white blanket of snow had turned her otherwise drab backyard into a winter wonderland. Avery's white Christmas was just two days away. Not that Avery would know or care now.

Betty looked beyond the fence toward

Jack's house and was surprised to see that the pink toilet, as well as a few other things, had been removed from his backyard. Perhaps he had taken her comments to heart and made that trip to the dump after all. But when would he have done that? Last night? It seemed a little odd to make a trip to the dump on a dark, snowy night. Was the dump even open? And why the big rush?

Unless Jack had something else he needed to dispose of…something like criminal evidence.

Betty shook her head as if to shake away these horrible thoughts. She was being foolish. Katie's talk of psychopaths and murderers had poisoned her mind. Jack was a good man. He had befriended Avery when she had no one to turn to. He had helped her out of a crisis. Betty should be very grateful. Not suspicious.

Betty jumped when the phone rang. Her heart raced as she picked it up. *Please, let nothing be wrong.* To her relief, it was Gary. And he sounded cheerful. "I checked the bus schedules, Mom," he said. "And it looks like Avery will be here in time for the Christmas Eve party tomorrow night."

"Oh, that's good." Betty sighed. "Did she call you?"

"No, but Steph thinks she's probably planning to surprise us. You know how unpredictable she can be."

"Oh, yes…of course."

"So it looks like our Christmas won't be spoiled after all."

"Oh, I'm so glad." Betty tried to insert a smile into her voice.

"Thanks for your help with this, Mom. We're just going into church now, so I'll have to hang up."

"Thank you for calling, dear."

When they hung up, Betty just sighed. Why was she feeling so emotional these days? Was it old age? The time of year? Senility?

She went into her bedroom to get ready for church. She always looked forward to the Christmas Sunday service. Their church didn't have an actual Christmas Eve or Christmas Day service like some did. But the Sunday prior to Christmas, they always did up right. At least that was something to look forward to.

Betty put on her favorite winter skirt, a red and black tartan plaid that Marsha had gotten for her in Scotland many years ago. Perhaps that had been the Deerwoods' twenty-fifth anniversary trip. She topped the skirt with a black cashmere sweater that had seen better days, then went to the bureau and opened her old jewelry box. But instead of retrieving her pearls, she paused to pick up an old photo of Chuck. He'd just enlisted in the army when it was taken. As hard as it was to see him leaving for Korea, she'd thought he looked so devastatingly handsome in that uniform. And when he'd offered her an engagement ring and the promise of marriage upon his return, she couldn't resist.

She studied his gentle brown eyes now and sighed. All these years later, she still got a sweet, warm feeling just looking into those eyes. So much love, compassion, tenderness… Oh, how she missed him. But, she reminded herself, each passing year brought her closer to their reunion.

She replaced the photo on the lace runner and sighed. She picked up her pearls (the ones Chuck had brought her from the Orient) and put them around her neck, checking the clasp to make sure it was connected.

As she went to the hall closet for her wool coat, she was still remembering Chuck's eyes. For some strange reason—and it almost seemed disrespectful—something about her dearly departed husband's eyes made her think of that stray mutt, Ralph. Oh, she knew there was no real relationship between the two. But something about the mutt's eyes—maybe just the color or maybe even the warmth—reminded her of Chuck.

As she got into her car, she wondered what Chuck would think of an old woman who abandoned homeless dogs at the pound just days before Christmas. More than that, she wondered what she thought about such things herself—not that she cared to think about it anymore.

She drove slowly to church, relieved to find that the main streets had been plowed, and told herself it was ridiculous to think along these lines. Imagining that her dearly departed husband would want her to take in a stray dog was not simply ridiculous, it bordered on the verge of crazy. Perhaps even a symptom of early Alzheimer's or dementia, although she certainly hoped not. But silly enough anyway.

Betty arrived early for church. She knew that the sanctuary could be crowded during the holidays, and she wanted to be able to sit in her regular spot. But when she got to the third row, she was dismayed to see that not only was her place taken, but so were the places where Jim and Marsha usually sat. She knew her disappointment was childish, not to mention selfish, and that the fourth row would be just fine. But feeling displaced as well as old, she simply turned around, went to the rear of the church, and sat in the very back row. Alone.

She told herself she would not feel sorry for herself as the organ played Christmas hymns. She forced a smile, or what she hoped might pass as a smile. She leaned back and closed her eyes and just listened to the music. After a couple of pieces, the choir began to sing. And soon the seats around her filled up, and although she didn't know the people sitting next to her, there was a comfort in being invisible in the midst of strangers.

During the first part of the Christmas service, which was much the same as every year, she continued to feel distracted as she pondered over what it was in Chuck's eyes that had brought that silly dog to mind. Well, besides plain foolishness. She sat up straighter and forced herself to focus on the children, who were dressed for the nativity story and singing "Silent Night." She remembered when her own children did this very same thing during their grade school years. Gary had always wanted to be a shepherd, and one year, not long after Chuck had passed, their own Susan was chosen to play Mary. So long ago. So far away.

Betty used her clean hanky to dab her eyes. She had quit keeping count of how many times she'd cried this past week, and simply decided that it was just a new stage in aging. And that her best defense was to keep a handkerchief handy.

Pastor Gordon was at the pulpit now, and Betty willed herself to listen. He'd been the pastor of this church for more than two decades, and Betty had grown to respect him for both his biblical knowledge and his spiritual insights. She had missed the beginning of his Christmas sermon but was determined to listen carefully for the remainder.

"It was not so different then, more than two thousand years ago." He nodded toward the children dressed in their robes and angel wings, who now sat restlessly in the front row. "At the first nativity, the world was not expecting this holy guest either. They were not prepared to receive this heavenly visitor, this stranger who came in the form of an innocent child. A babe, a gift from God Almighty. And yet the world needed him. They needed this gift—desperately.

"We are no different today, friends. We get caught up in the season, busily making preparations for Christmas. We decorate, bake cookies, shop, and wrap presents, and yet we aren't truly ready. We aren't waiting with great expectations. Our hearts aren't prepared to receive this holy guest, this heavenly visitor. We have already settled into our preconceived notions. We have decided how this thing called Christmas is about to go down. We have our agendas, we've made our plans." He chuckled. "But you know what they say about the plans of mice and men."

Pastor Gordon leaned over the pulpit and paused, looking across the congregation as if he were about to disclose a great secret. "God's ways are higher than our ways, my friends." He held up a fist and raised his voice. "And God's love can come unexpectedly. It can rock your life and rattle your heart! Just like the world wasn't ready to receive God's love in the form of a child that was hurled from heaven to earth, we're not always ready to receive God's love. And we're not prepared to accept that it comes in a variety of ways.

Often when we least expect it, God's love can show up in the form of something or someone we aren't happy to see—something or someone we want to push away or even run from. And, let me tell you, God's love can make us downright uncomfortable at times. Just like that newborn baby wailing in the night made some people in Bethlehem uncomfortable. And yet they needed him—desperately. And we need him. Desperately. Embrace God's love, my friends. Receive it. And then share it. Let us pray."

As Pastor Gordon prayed, Betty could think of only one thing. She had to get out of there. It wasn't that she wanted to escape her pastor or her friends or even the strangers sitting next to her. But what she wanted—what she truly, truly wanted—was to go straight to the animal shelter and get Ralph. Because it seemed entirely possible that God's love had come to her in the form of an unwanted little dog. And she had missed it. Oh, she'd probably missed lots of other things too. But she could do something about this. Ralph needed her, and she needed him.

When the service ended, she exchanged some hasty Christmas greetings and made her way to the exit, then left as quickly as she could. As she drove across town, she had no idea whether or not the shelter would even be open, but she was determined to find out. To her delight, the shelter was not only open, but Christmas music was playing and there were cookies out on the counter, and several people appeared to be shopping for pets. It was actually a very merry place.

Betty munched a sugar cookie as she waited for someone to help her.

"You're certainly busy," she said to the young man wearing a Santa hat who had just stepped behind the counter.

"That's because we had a spot on the local news this morning," he said. "We encouraged families to adopt unwanted animals rather than buying them from pet shops, which might support puppy farms where animals are not treated humanely."

"That's wonderful," Betty said.

"Except that we suggested they wait until *after* Christmas. But I guess we can't complain when our animals are finding good homes."

"No, of course not."

"So, what can we do for you? A cat perhaps? I have a nice tabby—"

"No thank you," she said. "I have something very specific in mind." She explained about dropping off Ralph recently. "It was a mistake, I'm afraid. And I'd like to have him back, if it's all right."

"Could you spot him?" the young man asked.

She smiled. "Of course."

He took her back to where dogs were barking and jumping in kennels. They walked up and down the aisle, and she studied all the dogs and finally shook her head. "I don't see him."

Just then the young woman who had helped her before walked by. Betty touched her arm and explained who she was and what she was looking for.

"Oh, that little brown terrier mix." The girl nodded. "Yes, he's been adopted."

Betty blinked. "Adopted?" Ralph had been adopted? How could this possibly happen?

The girl smiled. "Yes. He's such a sweet little dog, I'm not surprised someone wanted him. Now if you'll excuse me, I need to help this family with their paperwork."

"We have lots of other cool dogs," the young man said.

"Oh, yes…I see that you do." Betty just nodded.

"How about that schnauzer mix over—"

"No thank you."

"Are you sure?"

"Perhaps you're right about waiting until after the holidays…" She attempted to smile.

"Oh, yeah." He nodded. "It's better for the animal. So much is going on at Christmas. Pets get sick eating rich food or ornaments, or they get neglected or handled too much by guests—all kinds of holiday things that can be a threat to a new pet. You're wise to wait."

She thanked the young man for his help and then walked slowly out to her car. As she drove home, she tried to understand this whole strange chain of events. To start with, a dog she had never wanted and did not need had sneaked into her life. She had made many attempts to get rid of him and finally was successful. Or so she had thought. But as a result of dumping the dog—and wasn't that what she'd done?—she had hurt and then lost her granddaughter. Of course, she had wanted Avery to go home to her parents. But she hadn't wanted her to leave like that—not without at least saying good-bye. And what was the reason Betty had wanted Avery to leave? Jack. She had been fearful of Jack. She'd felt Avery would be safer at home.

Betty just shook her head to think of what a foolish woman she'd been.

And then she thought she'd figured things out while listening to Pastor Gordon's sermon—she knew that what she really wanted, what she needed, was that little dog. But now Ralph was gone. Adopted by someone else.

Love had come scratching at Betty's door in the form of a little brown dog, and she had completely missed it. She'd had her chance to welcome it, to receive it, and she had slammed the door in its face.

Chapter Fifteen

Betty woke up on Christmas Eve morning to the jarring sound of the phone ringing. It wasn't even seven yet, but she reached for the phone and tried to sound somewhat awake. "Hello?"

"Mom, this is Gary."

"Oh, Gary." She blinked and sat up. "How are you?"

"Not very well."

"Oh dear, what's wrong?"

"Steph was worried about Avery coming on that bus, afraid she wasn't going to get here in time or miss a connection. So I gave the route and schedule information to a cop friend of mine, and he checked the passenger list just to make sure everything was okay. And guess what?"

"I can't imagine."

"Avery was not a passenger."

"Oh?"

"She never even bought a ticket."

Betty was out of bed now. On her feet and pacing. "How can that be?"

"That's what we want to know. Where is Avery?"

"Goodness, I have no idea where she is, Gary."

"When did you last see her?"

Betty replayed the last several days for him, finally telling him about Ralph and how Avery had been hurt when she'd taken him to the shelter. "I was going to tell you this earlier," she said, "but I didn't want you to worry."

"We're worried now."

"I'm sorry."

"So who is this neighbor who supposedly put her on the bus?"

"Well, he didn't actually put her on the bus—"

"Who is he, Mom?"

"He lives in the old Spencer house. His name is Jack, and—"

"Crazy Jack?"

"What?"

"Susan told me you had a nutty neighbor who was tearing up his house and that you planned to move as soon as possible."

"Susan told you that?"

"Well, I might be exaggerating. We talked before she and Tim left for the Keys. She seemed to think the whole thing was rather humorous. I thought it sounded pretty bizarre. And I think you should sell your house."

"But I was wrong about Jack."

"How do you know?"

"Because I talked to him on Saturday. He helped Avery."

"Helped Avery do *what*?" Gary's voice was loud now. And sharp.

"He loaned her money and—"

"How do you know that, Mom? Did you *talk* to Avery?"

"Well, no."

"I'm sorry, Mom. I'm not mad at you. I know this isn't your fault. I'm just very frustrated. And Steph is coming unglued."

"I'm sorry." Betty didn't know what more to say. "But as you know, Avery has a mind and a will of her own. And she's not a child, Gary."

"Yes, so you've told me before."

"And I'm sure she's perfectly fine."

"I wish I felt as sure as you do." He sighed loudly. "My cop friend is going to help me figure out a way to look for her. We'll let you know if we find anything out. You do the same."

They said good-bye, and as she hung up, Betty felt her legs shaking as if they were going to give way. She sat down on her bed and just shook her head. What was going on? Where was Avery? And why didn't she get on that bus? Nothing made any sense. And now Betty was feeling frightened—and guilty. If anything had happened to Avery, if Jack was somehow to blame, Betty wouldn't be able to forgive herself.

She quickly got dressed, then pulled on her jacket and snow boots and walked toward Jack's house. But as she turned the corner, she saw that his pickup was gone. She stood there for a couple of minutes wondering what to do, and then she realized there was really nothing more she could do right now. Except pray.

As she trudged back to her house, she prayed for Avery—that she would be safe and that she would reveal her whereabouts to her family. Next she prayed for Ralph— that he'd found a good home and people who would love him. And finally she prayed for

Jack. Or maybe she prayed more for herself. She asked God to show her how to be a good neighbor to Jack. Then, as if adding a postscript, she said, "And, dear Lord, if Jack is a dangerous criminal, please show me the best way to inform the authorities so that he might be arrested. Amen."

Now she realized that sounded like a doubtful sort of prayer. How could one pray to love her neighbor with one breath and then pray about turning him in with the next? She just hoped that God would understand.

Betty went into her house and sat down at the kitchen table to make a grocery list. It wasn't that she wanted to go to the store, but she was out of necessities like bread, milk, eggs, and even coffee. And although she didn't feel the least bit hungry, she knew the responsible thing was to take care of this chore.

But after the sparse list was made, she just sat there staring at it. She felt as if all energy had been drained from her, as if it were an enormous chore simply to stand. Yet somehow she forced herself up. Then she stood there for a moment, feeling disoriented. Finally, she went into her bedroom and climbed into her bed, fully clothed, then pulled the covers up and slipped into a deep sleep.

"Grandma!"

Betty looked up and blinked. There before her stood Avery. At least Betty thought it sounded like Avery. But this girl was dressed in white and hovered over her like…like an angel. Was it an angel? Or was it Avery? Betty squinted her eyes, but the bright light behind the girl framed her head like a halo and made it hard to see. "Avery?"

"Are you okay, Grandma?"

Betty nodded and sat up. "Avery?" she said again.

"I'm sorry if I scared you." Avery sat down on the side of Betty's bed and reached for her hand. "Actually, you scared me. I knocked on the door and no one answered. And then I saw it was unlocked, which made me really worried, so I came in. And then I found you in bed like this and I thought…" Avery shook her head. "I thought you were dead."

Betty smiled and squeezed Avery's hand. "Not quite dead—just a little rattled and tired I suppose. But I'm better now."

Avery hugged her. "I'm so sorry I was such a spoiled brat."

"You?" Betty held on to the girl. "I'm the one who should be sorry."

Avery released Betty and studied her face. "Why should *you* be sorry?"

Betty reached out to touch Avery's cheek, wanting to make sure she was real and not just a dream. "I have so many reasons to be sorry, Avery. Where do I begin?"

"With a cup of tea?" Avery suggested.

Betty nodded. "Yes, that sounds perfect."

"I'll go get it started."

"I'm right behind you." Betty stood and slipped on her shoes, then hurried into the kitchen, where Avery was already filling the kettle.

"I still can't believe it's you," Betty said. She watched Avery turn on the stove and reach for the tea mugs and tea canister. "I saw a girl dressed in white…" She chuckled. "And I thought that God had sent an angel to get me."

Avery laughed. "I'm hardly an angel. And this ugly white blouse is my uniform."

"Uniform?"

"Yeah. I got a job at the bus station café."

"The bus station café?" Betty sat down in a kitchen chair.

"Yes. It's a long story. I was so furious at

you for giving Ralph away that I ran off to Jack's house and unloaded on him. I told him I was leaving that night, but he talked me into waiting until morning."

"And then he loaned you money and took you to the bus station?"

"Did you talk to him?"

"Yes. I was worried."

"He's really a sweet guy, Grandma. He even tried to talk me into staying with you. But I told him I was done with you." Avery made a sad smile. "I'm sorry."

"Don't worry, I understand. I've been a bit fed up with myself too."

"So anyway, I was at the bus station and about to get a ticket to take me home, but I just couldn't stand the idea of going back there. So I got a cup of coffee."

"At the bus station café?"

"Exactly. This girl was the only waitress there. And she was in the weeds."

"In the weeds?"

"You know, too many customers, too many orders, over her head."

"Oh. I see."

"And everyone was complaining, and this one dude was being really rude to her because his cheeseburger was probably getting cold, and she was about to start crying."

"Poor thing."

"That's what I thought, so I walked right past her and got his cheeseburger and handed it to him. And then I started taking orders and getting stuff and filling coffee cups, and the girl never even questioned it."

"Really?" Betty tried not to look too stunned. What nerve!

"Finally, it kind of slowed down, and the girl asked me who I was and if I'd come about the job." Avery put the teabags in the mugs.

"And so she hired you?"

"Her dad did. He's the cook and the manager. They'd just lost two waitresses earlier that week. And with holiday travelers, they were getting desperate."

"But how did you know how to do all that?" Betty studied Avery. "Taking orders and getting food. Don't you need to be trained or licensed or something?"

"Waitressing is waitressing. I've done it a lot of times." She filled the mugs with hot water and brought them over to the table.

"But it's been two nights since you left. Where did you stay?"

"Abby and Carl let me sleep on their couch."

"The waitress and the cook?"

"Yeah. But that couch was getting uncomfortable. And Abby's sister Laurel was coming home from school today, so the apartment was going to be crowded. They gave me tonight and tomorrow off since Laurel will help them out. So I thought I'd come check on you. Then you scared me half to death by playing possum in your bed. Were you feeling sick?"

"Just very tired." Betty took a slow sip of tea.

"Hey, how did you like my decorations for the anniversary party?"

Betty gushed about how much she loved them and how everyone else was extremely impressed as well. "Marsha and Jim were completely overwhelmed with how beautiful it was, and their grandchildren thought you must be a professional artist."

"I wish."

"So, do you want to continue with the waitress job?" Betty asked.

"Yeah. For a while. Until I figure something else out."

"Would you like to stay here?" Betty asked. "The city bus stop is only—"

"Two blocks from here." Avery grinned.

"You know that you're welcome."

"Thanks. I'd appreciate it."

"Would you mind calling your parents?"
Avery frowned.

"Or, if you don't mind, I can call them—
just so they'll know you're safe."

"That's okay. I'll call them. I'm trying to
act more like a grown-up. That's what Jack
told me I should do."

"He told you that?"

"And a lot of other things. He's been
through a lot, Grandma. You should get to
know him better. I think you'll like him."

Betty nodded. "I'm sure you're right."

They finished their tea, and Avery, true to
her word, called her mother. Betty could hear
the tension in Avery's voice, and not wanting
to eavesdrop, she hurried back into her bedroom and closed the door.

"It's safe to come out now," Avery called
after a few minutes.

"I take it your mother wasn't too happy."

"That's a pretty safe guess."

"But she was relieved to hear you're okay?"

"I suppose."

"It's not easy being a parent, Avery."

Avery just shrugged with a hurt expression, and Betty decided to change the subject. "You'll never guess what I did yesterday."

"Let's see. It was Sunday…did you go to church?"

Betty smiled. "Yes, as a matter of fact, I did. But after that I went to the animal shelter. I wanted to get Ralph."

Avery's eyes lit up. "You got him back?"

Betty sighed. "No. I was too late. Someone else adopted him."

Now Avery looked sadder than ever.

"I'm sorry," Betty said quickly. "Maybe I shouldn't have told you that. But I just wanted you to know that I had a complete change of heart. I realized that Ralph was a wonderful, sweet little dog. And that I needed him. It almost seemed like God had sent him to me, and then I'd stupidly turned him away. I can't even describe how sad that made me feel." She put a hand on Avery's shoulder. "Almost as sad as losing you."

"But I'm back."

"Yes, you are." Betty smiled. "And I need to go to the grocery store. I made a short list, but now that you're here, I think it's time to kill the fattened calf."

Avery looked confused.

"Or roast a turkey."

So they went to the grocery store, and since Betty had already spent her December budget, she decided to dip into January's. Of course, this would blow her grocery budget to pieces. But she didn't even care.

Chapter Sixteen

"This is a lot of food, Grandma." Avery surveyed the bags now lined up like soldiers on the kitchen counter.

Betty chuckled. "Well, yes, I suppose it is. We better get those cold items in the fridge."

"Can we invite Jack for Christmas dinner?" Avery handed Betty the turkey. "I mean, if he doesn't have other plans, which I'll bet he doesn't since he has no family around here anymore."

"Anymore?" Betty adjusted the lower shelf to make room for the turkey.

"Yeah. Jack's grandparents used to own his house."

"Jack's grandparents?" Betty scowled. "The only people who've ever lived in that house were the Spencers."

"Yeah. They must've been Jack's mom's parents. He said she grew up here. He even showed me her room. It's still painted pink."

"Donna Spencer is Jack's mom?" Betty dropped the package of celery in the vegetable bin and turned to stare at Avery. "Are you sure?"

"You know Jack's mom?"

"I knew her. Donna was a sweet girl. As a teenager, she used to babysit my children during the summers when I worked at the post office. Then she got married and moved away. Last time I saw her, she was on her second marriage." Betty strained her memory. "It seems to me that she had a little boy in her second marriage, but they only came out to visit a few times. And I think his name was Johnny."

"Jack."

"Jack is Johnny?"

"Yeah. I guess he switched over to Jack while he was in Afghanistan."

"He was in Afghanistan?"

Avery nodded and handed Betty a bag of potatoes. "He said it was pretty rough over there. But it sounds like it's been almost as rough being home. He told me he has horrible nightmares, and that's why he likes to work on his house at night sometimes."

"Oh." Betty still remembered how Chuck had had bad dreams after he'd come back from Korea, but he'd never wanted to talk about his experience there. And to think Jack had been suffering too. Making noise in the night, with his neighbors all thinking the worst of him. She shook her head. "Poor boy."

"Anyway, his mom gave him that house," Avery said.

"Donna gave him the house?"

"Yeah. She and her brother inherited it. Only her brother didn't want it."

Betty just shook her head. "I still can't believe I didn't know that Jack was Gladys and Al's grandson. I wish he would've told me sooner."

Avery shrugged. "It sounds like he never got the chance."

"I suppose I never gave him the chance."

They were done putting things away now. "I think it's a lovely idea to invite Jack for Christmas dinner," Betty said. "How about if we invite the Gilmores too, unless they're busy. It's about time neighbors started getting acquainted."

"And we can serve dinner in the dining

room," Avery said. "We'll use your pretty dishes. I'll get it all set up and—" Avery paused. "Can you hear that, Grandma?"

Betty stopped folding the paper bag and listened. "My old ears aren't too sharp."

"It sounds like someone at the door."

Betty tucked the bag into a drawer, then looked up in time to see Avery dashing out of the kitchen. "Grandma!" she screamed. "Com'ere quick!"

Frightened that there was an armed gunman at the door, Betty hurried to see Avery squatting on the floor with a familiar little brown dog licking her face.

"It's Ralph!" Avery said. "He's back!"

Betty couldn't believe her eyes. But it certainly did look like Ralph. "How on earth?"

"He found us, Grandma!" Avery scooped the dog into her arms. "He's home!"

Betty considered this. On many levels she wanted to agree with her granddaughter and say, "Yes, he's home, and all will be well." But at the same time, she was concerned. "But the people at the shelter said he'd been adopted, Avery."

"Maybe he didn't like his new owners."

Betty nodded. "Maybe."

"Can we keep him?"

"You know I want to keep him, Avery. But what if his new owners are looking for him right now? I'm sure they paid good money for him. He was probably meant to be someone's Christmas present. And certainly there's some kind of record at the shelter—"

"So what are you saying?"

"I'm saying that I'd better call the shelter. I'll explain everything to them, and I'll ask if we might possibly purchase Ralph back from his new owners. The shelter people care about animals, and I'm sure they'll understand that Ralph came looking for us, not the other way around. Ralph is more than welcome to stay with us, Avery, but I do think we need to go about this the right way."

Avery looked disappointed, but at least she agreed. Betty went to make the call. She carefully explained everything right from the beginning until how the dog had shown up of his own free will this afternoon. "I'm sure his new owners must be worried," Betty finished. "If I knew their phone number, I could give them a call." Betty decided not to mention her ulterior motive about wanting to purchase Ralph back from his new family.

"I can understand your problem," the woman said. "We're a little shorthanded here today. But if it will help to reunite the dog to his family, I think it's okay for me to give you the name and phone number of the dog's owner."

"Thank you so much!"

The woman shared the information, and Betty thanked her and hung up.

"So?" Avery was waiting expectantly.

Betty just stood there, staring first at the dog and then at Avery.

"What's wrong, Grandma?"

"The owner…" Betty shook her head. "It's Jack."

"Our Jack?"

Betty nodded.

Avery sighed. "Oh."

"I had no idea Jack wanted the dog."

"He didn't."

"Well, to be fair, neither did I." Betty sighed. "Not at first."

Avery was clearly disappointed, but she just nodded. "Fine. I'll take Ralph back to Jack. Just let me run and use the bathroom first."

Betty reached down and patted Ralph's head. "It was nice of you to pop in to say hello," she said. "At least we're neighbors. And you're welcome to visit—"

Just then there was a loud knock on the door. Betty opened it to see Jack standing there. "Come on in, Jack."

He came in hesitantly. "Sorry to disturb you, Betty, but I'm, uh, looking for—" His brows lifted slightly when he noticed the dog. "Looks like Ralph decided to drop by."

Betty nodded. "And I just found out that he belongs to you now."

Jack looked slightly sheepish. "I just couldn't bear to think of him at the pound."

"He's a good dog."

Jack actually smiled now. "He is a good dog. But he seems a little confused about where he lives today."

Avery came into the room with her parka and bag over one arm. "Jack!"

"Avery!" Jack looked even happier to see her than she was to see him. "What are you doing here?"

With half sentences tumbling over each other, Avery explained about not going home, her new job, and her decision to stay in town. "Which reminds me, I want to pay you back the loan now."

He waved his hand. "That's okay, you—"

"No way," she said quickly, reaching for her bag. "I'm trying to do the grown-up, responsible thing. Remember?" She counted out the money into his hand. "Sorry about all the change, it's from tips. And you'll have to trust me for that last twenty. I had to use it for a city bus pass."

"Well, I better get out of your hair." Jack reached down to pick up Ralph. "Sorry to have bothered you."

"It's no bother," Betty said quickly. "In fact, we wanted to invite you for Christmas dinner tomorrow."

"Grandma got a turkey and all the trimmings." Avery smiled. "And I'm going to make a pumpkin pie."

"Do you have plans?" Betty asked.

"No…"

"Then we'll expect you at two."

Jack nodded. "All right then."

"And bring Ralph too," Avery said.

Jack chuckled. "My guess is that he'll beat me over here."

Chapter Seventeen

Jack guessed right. Shortly before noon on Christmas Day, Ralph came over to visit them again. "He must've smelled the turkey cooking," Avery told Betty. She led the little dog into the kitchen, then returned to where she'd been rolling out pie dough.

"Merry Christmas, Ralph." Betty plucked a turkey giblet out of the dressing she was mixing and tossed it to him.

"You're too early for dinner," Avery told him.

"Should we take him back?" Betty asked.

Avery paused with the rolling pin in her hand. "I suppose that's the right thing to do, Grandma. Although I'll bet Jack can guess where he is."

"How about if I take him," Betty offered

as she wiped her hands on her apron. "That way you can finish the pie crust before it dries out. And I wanted to give Jack another cookie plate anyway."

Betty put together a generous goodie platter, but instead of putting the red bow on the plastic wrap like she usually did, she stuck it on Ralph's head. "Come on, boy," she called as she went for her coat. Acting as if he'd received top honors at doggy obedience school, Ralph stuck to her heels as she led him out the front door and down the walk.

Betty smiled as the little dog took the lead, trotting about a foot in front of her like he knew exactly where he was going and why. He turned the corner and headed straight to Jack's house just like he lived there. And, well, didn't he? Still, as Betty followed him, she couldn't help but wonder how a little stray dog like that had wandered into their lives, or how he had attached himself to not just one person in need, but two. Make that three. And she considered how this little dog had brought them all together. Really, in some ways, it seemed nothing short of a miracle.

"Merry Christmas," she told Jack when he opened the door.

"Hey, I was just looking for you, Ralphie."

Jack grinned to see the red bow on his dog's head. "You're like a real party animal."

"He's a very special dog," Betty said. She handed Jack the cookies. "I think he just likes bringing people together."

"I guess so." Jack's expression grew thoughtful. "You know, Betty, I was wondering if it would be okay for me to give Ralph to Avery for Christmas. I know how much she loves him and everything. But then I got worried that you might not appreciate that—you might not want a dog in your house. And I sure don't want to rock your boat again."

Betty just laughed. "You know what I think, Jack?"

He looked slightly bewildered now. "What?"

"I think Ralph is a Christmas dog, and I think he's going to give himself to whoever he feels needs him the most."

Jack nodded. "I think you're right. Kinda like share the love?"

"And maybe we'll just have to share him too."

"Tell you what, Betty." Jack nodded toward the backyard. "I'm going to rebuild that fence—right where it's standing now, where my grandparents built it—but how about if we put a gate between the two yards?"

"And a doggy door too?"

"Absolutely." He stuck out his hand. "Deal?"

"It's a deal." Betty firmly shook his hand, then opened her arms to hug him, nearly toppling his cookie platter. "Welcome to the neighborhood, Jack!"

"Thanks, Betty. I think I'm starting to feel at home."

Betty patted Ralph's head again. "I thank you, little Christmas dog, for bringing us all together. And now I have a turkey to baste."

"We'll see you at two," Jack called. "Merry Christmas!"

"Merry Christmas," she called back. As she walked toward home, it occurred to her that her old neighborhood—which looked more spectacular than ever in its clean white blanket of fresh, fallen snow—was getting better all the time.

* * * * *

REQUEST YOUR FREE BOOKS!

2 FREE RIVETING INSPIRATIONAL NOVELS
PLUS 2 FREE MYSTERY GIFTS

Love Inspired®
SUSPENSE

YES! Please send me 2 FREE Love Inspired® Suspense novels and my 2 FREE mystery gifts (gifts are worth about $10). After receiving them, if I don't wish to receive any more books, I can return the shipping statement marked "cancel." If I don't cancel, I will receive 4 brand-new novels every month and be billed just $4.74 per book in the U.S. or $5.24 per book in Canada. That's a savings of at least 21% off the cover price. It's quite a bargain! Shipping and handling is just 50¢ per book in the U.S. and 75¢ per book in Canada.* I understand that accepting the 2 free books and gifts places me under no obligation to buy anything. I can always return a shipment and cancel at any time. Even if I never buy another book, the two free books and gifts are mine to keep forever.

123/323 IDN F5AN

Name	(PLEASE PRINT)	

Address		Apt. #

City	State/Prov.	Zip/Postal Code

Signature (if under 18, a parent or guardian must sign)

Mail to the Harlequin® Reader Service:
IN U.S.A.: P.O. Box 1867, Buffalo, NY 14240-1867
IN CANADA: P.O. Box 609, Fort Erie, Ontario L2A 5X3

**Are you a current subscriber to Love Inspired Suspense books
and want to receive the larger-print edition?
Call 1-800-873-8635 or visit www.ReaderService.com.**

* Terms and prices subject to change without notice. Prices do not include applicable taxes. Sales tax applicable in N.Y. Canadian residents will be charged applicable taxes. Offer not valid in Quebec. This offer is limited to one order per household. Not valid for current subscribers to Love Inspired Suspense books. All orders subject to credit approval. Credit or debit balances in a customer's account(s) may be offset by any other outstanding balance owed by or to the customer. Please allow 4 to 6 weeks for delivery. Offer available while quantities last.

Your Privacy—The Harlequin® Reader Service is committed to protecting your privacy. Our Privacy Policy is available online at www.ReaderService.com or upon request from the Harlequin Reader Service.
We make a portion of our mailing list available to reputable third parties that offer products we believe may interest you. If you prefer that we not exchange your name with third parties, or if you wish to clarify or modify your communication preferences, please visit us at www.ReaderService.com/consumerschoice or write to us at Harlequin Reader Service Preference Service, P.O. Box 9062, Buffalo, NY 14269. Include your complete name and address.

LISDIR13R

REQUEST YOUR FREE BOOKS!

2 FREE INSPIRATIONAL NOVELS
PLUS 2
FREE
MYSTERY GIFTS

Love Inspired.
HISTORICAL
INSPIRATIONAL HISTORICAL ROMANCE

YES! Please send me 2 FREE Love Inspired® Historical novels and my 2 FREE mystery gifts (gifts are worth about $10). After receiving them, if I don't wish to receive any more books, I can return the shipping statement marked "cancel." If I don't cancel, I will receive 4 brand-new novels every month and be billed just $4.74 per book in the U.S. or $5.24 per book in Canada. That's a savings of at least 21% off the cover price. It's quite a bargain! Shipping and handling is just 50¢ per book in the U.S. and 75¢ per book in Canada.* I understand that accepting the 2 free books and gifts places me under no obligation to buy anything. I can always return a shipment and cancel at any time. Even if I never buy another book, the two free books and gifts are mine to keep forever.

102/302 IDN F5CY

Name	(PLEASE PRINT)	

Address		Apt. #

City	State/Prov.	Zip/Postal Code

Signature (if under 18, a parent or guardian must sign)

Mail to the Harlequin® Reader Service:
IN U.S.A.: P.O. Box 1867, Buffalo, NY 14240-1867
IN CANADA: P.O. Box 609, Fort Erie, Ontario L2A 5X3

Want to try two free books from another series?
Call 1-800-873-8635 or visit www.ReaderService.com.

* Terms and prices subject to change without notice. Prices do not include applicable taxes. Sales tax applicable in N.Y. Canadian residents will be charged applicable taxes. Offer not valid in Quebec. This offer is limited to one order per household. Not valid for current subscribers to Love Inspired Historical books. All orders subject to credit approval. Credit or debit balances in a customer's account(s) may be offset by any other outstanding balance owed by or to the customer. Please allow 4 to 6 weeks for delivery. Offer available while quantities last.

Your Privacy—The Harlequin® Reader Service is committed to protecting your privacy. Our Privacy Policy is available online at www.ReaderService.com or upon request from the Harlequin Reader Service.

We make a portion of our mailing list available to reputable third parties that offer products we believe may interest you. If you prefer that we not exchange your name with third parties, or if you wish to clarify or modify your communication preferences, please visit us at www.ReaderService.com/consumerschoice or write to us at Harlequin Reader Service Preference Service, P.O. Box 9062, Buffalo, NY 14269. Include your complete name and address.

LIHDIR13R